The Master
Part One
Target

Author: Simone Leigh

Copyright © 2019

All rights reserved. No part of this book may be reproduced or transmitted in any form or by any means, digital, mechanical, electronic including photocopying, recording or by any information storage or retrieval system without permission in writing from the author.

Target

Michael - Eleven Weeks

I lie awake, an arm propped behind my head. Lying beside me; Charlotte, eyes closed, her breathing steady and slow. Beyond her, James, the rise and fall of his chest equally regular.

Richard and Beth are in the next room. Perhaps they're sleeping. I'm not sure. It seems to me I sometimes hear a low murmur of words.

But, my mind a-whirl, sleep escapes me.

Should I get up?

Make a coffee? Read perhaps...

But right now, I don't want to leave the bed or my sleeping wife. For her perhaps to wake and find me not here.

So, tossing and turning, I while away the darkness, watching slanted moonbeams make their slow progression across the carpet, then the bed, before finally fading. And now the first grey light of dawn creeps across the windows.

A blackbird chirrups its early arpeggio; a sweet melodic prelude to the full chorus that will follow.

And still my mind wheels and turns.

The sheer enormity of what Richard has offered me takes my breath away.

Beth.

Beautiful, sweet, submissive Beth. So like my own Charlotte physically. But so unlike in her every other way.

Richard's wife. His submissive. So much younger than he is.

And he has... What? *Bequeathed* her to me?

A second wife?

And Charlotte says she doesn't mind. Even encourages it.

As does James.

Why?

I roll onto my side, settling to watch my sleeping flame-haired beauty.

And gradually, it dawns on me that her breathing is not the slow steady rhythm of the sleeper...

She's not asleep...

Pretending?

"Charlotte?"

Her eyes flick open. Not the gradual flutter of the slowly waking, but the snap of the already conscious. And her gaze settles on me. In the daylight, that gaze would be emerald, but now, in the early dawn, she is a pattern of light and shade; a tracery in grey, her eyes a white gleam.

She shifts, crisp linen sheets rustling in the semi-dark and her hand cups my cheek. "You okay?" She leans in, brushing her lips over mine.

"Shouldn't I be asking *you* that?"

Her body vibrates; quiet laughter. "I'm *fine*. Really, I am. Richard asked me before he spoke to you. So..." She strokes my face. "... *Are* you okay?"

"I'm not sure. It's hard to put into words..."

"Overwhelm?" A glint from her teeth joins that from her eyes.

"That's as good a description as any... Charlotte..."

"You're not changing your mind, are you? About Beth?"

"I'm... I don't know. Charlotte, are you *sure* you're alright about this? It's not every woman who'd be happy for her husband to have a second wife."

She chuckles. "It's not every man who would accept that his wife has two husbands. But you're right. If it were any other woman than Beth, no, I wouldn't have accepted it." The chuckle turns to a snort. "I'd have scratched her freakin' eyes out." Her voice softens. "But it *is* Beth..."

I reach for her, sliding an arm around her waist, pulling her, warm and yielding, to me

She snuggles close, contouring herself to my body, nuzzling into the nook of my neck and shoulder. "You smell good."

"Charlotte, I promised you on our wedding night that you would never have cause to regret marrying me."

"Yes, you did. And you never *have* given me cause."

"Not even now? A bit of partying with Richard and Beth on special occasions is one thing, but *this*..."

She pulls away, leaning back so she can look me in the face. "*Have* you changed your mind? Yesterday evening you agreed to it, but we were all there. If you said yes to Richard because you were feeling pressured or for the wrong reasons..."

"No, I wasn't pressured. That's not it. It's... you *did* all spring it on me. You obviously all knew about it before. You'd discussed it. I had two minutes' notice."

She sits up, knees hugging up to the slight swell of her belly, pulling the sheets to her chest. "If you want to change your mind, you should do it sooner rather than later. Beth and Richard would understand if it happened now. Later..."

"I don't want to change my mind... exactly... But I wanted to talk to you about it. Talk it through. Last night, we didn't discuss *anything*... There was no opportunity to discuss anything... About how it would work. Are we a... a *five-some*? Or are we an overlapping couple and our Triad. Who would live where? Or when might we all meet up Or... *anything*..."

"That's all detail."

"I know it's detail. We can work through it. But... but mainly... I have to be certain that *you* are alright with this."

"Michael, I've already..."

I cut her off, sitting up to look her in the eye. "Charlotte, I never expected to meet a woman where not only do I want to be faithful to her, I have no inclination to be otherwise. You never asked me to be faithful to you, but it's something I have always wanted to do for you. My gift to you. The only woman I've touched since you and I met is Beth herself, and you agreed, even encouraged that."

A finger of sunlight creeps across the carpet, the light turning from grey to golden. Her mouth twitches mischief. "How many have you had?"

"What? How many what?" I'm protesting, pretending innocence, but I understand exactly what she's asking. I simply don't want to answer her.

"Women. How many women have you had? Before me."

"I never counted."

The mischief dances into her eyes. "You never counted your conquests?"

"Women aren't conquests. And they're not numbers either."

She jerks a thumb to the sleeping James at her side. "Marcie said that the two of you had… what were her words? 'Worked every sub within twenty miles'…"

Fucking Marcie…

"How about your own past?"

Her forehead creases. "What about my past? You know how we met…" She colours up. "The Auction…"

"Yes, James bought you and he invited me in the following day. But after that week, you went to college. What happened there?"

"What do you mean? What happened?"

"You had no boyfriends at college? After that first week? You'd discovered you enjoyed sex."

"I… there were a couple. I had a date or two. But it never…" She stutters to a halt.

"I'm guessing it was a bit pale compared to what James and I give you?"

She nods down to her knees, looking forlorn. "Yes."

You bastard…

"Babe, I'm sorry if I embarrassed you. The fact is, I have a past. Everyone does."

"Do you miss it?"

"Miss what? Playing the field?"

"Yes. You had so much freedom when you were single and I wondered, maybe..."

"I think about it sometimes, but if by miss it, you mean, do I want to go back to that? No, I don't. I have you."

"And now Beth too."

"And now, Beth." Framing her face with my hands, "But that doesn't change in any way how I feel about you, or the fact that you are my wife and I am your husband."

"I know that." She smiles, leaning in to meet me half-way and we kiss.

She breaks off. "Ahh... damn."

"What?"

She pats her stomach. "I need to pee."

I shift to let her past and she climbs out of the bed, supporting her stomach with one hand and clutching at her breasts with the other. "I'm going to have to wear a bra in bed if these damn things get any bigger."

"They look pretty good to me. But I suspect they'll getter bigger than that. It's early days yet."

She gives me a slow look then vanishes off into the bathroom, leaving me with the 'sleeping' James.

"You're not fooling me. I know you're awake."

His eyes flick open, his mouth quirking with humour. "And have been for some time. I'll admit, I was enjoying the turn the conversation had taken. I would have liked to hear more."

"You didn't want to join in?"

"You had things you needed to say to Charlotte."

"You could say that, yes. You shared her with me, arranged that I married her and now you've conspired to give me a *second* wife. Competition for her affections."

He stares up for a moment, sucking at his cheeks. "I don't know that *conspired* is the right word..."

"Oh, I think it is."

He sniffs. "Alright, it is. In the same way that you and Charlotte arranged that her first child would be mine..."

"That's what friends do for each other."

"And *this* is what friends do for each other. There's no question between you and me of competition for Charlotte's affection. There's no jealousy between her and Beth. And you're perfectly capable of giving each of them what they need and deserve. We all had good reasons for the things we did."

He sits up, scraping at a blue haze of stubble. "No one should have to deal with what Ben did to you, for all that he convinced himself he was doing it on your behalf. Klempner had it right when he talked about betrayal."

Klempner...

Wonder where he is now?

*****

Thailand

At 'Arrivals', I wait, card clutched in hand: *Strohmayer Party*.

The crowds throng by, sweeping past; wives and husbands, lovers, and teenage sweethearts meet and embrace. Men smile, shake hands and slap backs, women hug and kiss cheeks. Children, olive-skinned, dark-haired and almond-eyed run to meet smiling oldsters, arms outstretched, shrieking as they run.

Nothing of this feels familiar.

But then, when did anyone come running to me?

My mother, a smile on her lips, laughter in her eyes, hunkering down, arms outstretched as I toddle to her, as fast as short legs will carry me... "Larry, Sweetheart..."

And **Him** in the background; *red-faced, scowling, bleary-eyed*.

Enough...

Ah... there they are...

Six in the group, middle-aged, prosperous and coming to 'party'...

... for a given definition of 'party'.

That's got to be them.

I adjust my cap to just the right angle, brush down the jacket and straighten up, making sure the card is prominent.

The leader of the group is scanning the crowd. His eyes settle on the card and he looks back, jerking his chin at me. He struts across...

Rich...

Arrogant...

Jerk...

"Mr Strohmayer?"

"You the chauffeur?" His voice is a nice mix of accent and condescension.

"I'm here to take you to your lodgings, sir, yes."

"Great." He thumbs to the back of the group where one of them pushes a trolley piled with what looks like baggage for the lot of them. "Cases are back there. You can take us to the car. Limo? As I ordered?"

"Yes, sir. Everything as you ordered. Air conditioning. Drinks in the chiller. Everything for your comfort. If there is anything..."

"Just get us out of this heat." He runs a finger around his collar. "Fucking humidity's got me already. It'd better be everything we were promised. We've paid a lot for this."

I duck my head and copy/paste my best tone of ingratiation. "I think, sir, I can guarantee you the experience of a lifetime."

"Good. Paid a fuckin' fortune for this. I want my money's worth."

In the car - a stretch-limo as ordered; "If there is anything else you want, sirs, or any questions, just..."

"How old are they?" pipes up one. "I'm not looking for some sixteen-year-old claiming to be fourteen. I want the real thing."

"You can choose, sir. Whatever you want. All ages. Both sexes. Local, foreign, Western, Asian, blond, dark. You name it. You'll find it."

"How young?" says one of them. He's got that seedy hue that comes from spending too much time indoors bending over a screen.

Probably dick-less and can't pull an actual woman...

"As young as you want, sir."

Dickless leans back and sighs. "Great. I want it really tight when I..."

"Alright," snaps Strohmayer. "We don't want to hear it, Frischmann. Whatever you want's gonna be there. Where are we eating?"

"I'm taking you there now, sir. A banquet for six laid on. A mix of traditional Thai and Western dishes as requested. Is there anything..."

"Shut the fuck up and give us some privacy."

"Of course, sir."

That works for me...

I tap the button raising the glass screen behind me, making sure I turn my face from the rear-view so they don't see me smiling.

Ain't the internet wonderful? All those people who, once, would have been so hard to find. Now, in these days of the great and glorious World Wide Web, you locate the right 'social media' on the dark-net and, *Hey, Presto...*

I turn off the main highway and down the track through the rainforest.

"What kind of hotel is this?" spouts one. His voice echoes through the intercom, tinny and reedy. I'm not sure how much of the tone is his own voice and how much the connection, but...

"Obviously sirs, even here, we have to be discreet. You understand that *technically* this is illegal, regardless of the realities and the consent of the children involved."

"They have consented, have they?" It's the runt who was pushing the baggage trolley when I met them.

"Or their parents have consented. Often, the children are supporting older members of their families through the work."

One of them discovers the drinks cabinet, starts splashing gin and tonic, malt and whatever else. It doesn't matter which they choose. There's enough Zolpidem in any of the bottles to incapacitate the drinkers.

As they clink glasses and exchange brags, I knock down the security lock. None of them notices.

*****

Michael - Eleven Weeks

In the kitchen, I find James extending the breakfast table. "Six for breakfast." His face is suspiciously straight. "We need more space."

Mitch joins us, heading for the jar containing her peppermint tea. She's wearing an expression which hovers between a twinkle and a question. She turns her gaze on Charlotte. "Yes?"

"Yes, Michael accepted."

Mitch nods, her expression thoughtful, then turns to help James set out the table. "I'll do that."

"Thanks." He collects eggs from the fridge... "A good breakfast all round, I think." Then brandishing a bottle, "And perhaps some bucks fizz by way of celebration."

"Sounds good to me." In truth, I feel a little awkward, pinned under Mitch's gaze. She's barely arrived with us, learning that her long lost daughter has two 'husbands', and now one of them has...

What?

... an *arrangement* that he has a second 'wife'.

But she doesn't look annoyed. Her mouth is twitching as she smooths the tablecloth. "You lead an adventurous life, don't you," she comments, taking cutlery from the drawer and laying out six sets.

"Are you alright with it? You obviously knew about it. And before I did too."

"I'm happy if Jenny is happy."

We're interrupted by the arrival of Beth and Richard, both casual in jeans and tee-shirts.

Richard, one hand in the small of Beth's back, gestures her to a chair. "Good morning, James, Michael. Good morning, Mitch."

Ignoring the heat on my cheeks, I take my place at the table, a seat between Charlotte and Beth. Beth meets my eye, then looks away, a flush rising up her neck.

At least it's not just me...

I give Charlotte a peck on the cheek as, bland faced, she butters a stack of toast then pushes the rack to Beth, who sits, eyes downcast, face pinking.

Charlotte speaks through a mouthful of crunch. "Aren't you going to kiss your new wife, 'Good morning'?" Beth's eyes roll to her, and back to me again.

"Morning, Beth." I give her a peck on the cheek too. The flush deepens, but she returns the kiss with a muttered 'Morning'.

Richard says nothing, simply cradling a steaming mug, but the devil dances in his eyes.

James bustles around the kitchen area. "What would you like for breakfast, Beth?"

"What Mitch is having looks nice."

"Coming up." James deposits cereal, a bowl of chopped fruit and yoghurt by her. Then he hovers over the table with the jug. "More coffee, Richard?"

Richard winces, then rises, heading for the hob. "No, thanks, James. I'll make another pot."

"No need. There's plenty."

Richard clicks his tongue. "I've tasted your coffee, James. And I value my stomach lining. I'll make my own."

The six of us around the table makes for a very convivial breakfast. Half an hour and about ten thousand calories later, we all settle back drinking tea, peppermint and coffee.

"Ah..." James tops up his horrendous brew. "So... where do we go from here?"

Where indeed?

Richard pours for himself from a second jug, then offers it to Beth. "I'd say, let's take things gradually. There's no need to force any kind of pace. However, our group relationship develops, there's no hurry. And we all have different lives." Putting his cup down, he steeples fingers.

"Whatever's going to happen between us, we should let it happen organically..."

Thank God for that...

Charlotte, wiping crumbs from her lips, mumbles agreement through a mouthful of egg. Beth follows. Mitch simply watches with a cool gaze.

Richard continues, "Just now we are two separate families, in two separate homes. Perhaps as a start, we should spend the occasional weekend with each other?"

"A good idea." James waves his coffee cup, punctuating his words, putting it down again as it slops over. "And I have another suggestion. How about a couple of weeks at the beach house? We're in June now. We could make arrangements, organize our workloads for some time off in July or August."

Richard arches his brows. "Sounds good to me. Elizabeth?"

She looks down, dimpling. "It sounds lovely." Her hand slips into mine, squeezing my fingers. I squeeze back.

"They do say," comments Mitch, "that the way to really find out if you get along with someone is to spend a holiday with them."

Richard nods into his coffee. "There's a lot of truth in that. And with what we are proposing with our 'family' of five, *plus* extras..." He nods down to first Beth's belly, then Charlotte's... "We'd better be sure we have something workable."

He pauses. "You're very quiet, Michael, considering *your* role in all this."

"Richard, I'm still reeling. But I'd say a vacation at the beach house is an excellent idea."

"Good. Mitch, will you join us?"

A porcelain cup poised between her fingers, she hesitates. "I don't think so, no. This is about the five of you. Whatever Jenny's life-choices are, it is for her to make them work. My being there would simply be interference."

James exchanges a glance with me, frowning. "Mitch, you're part of the family now. You're welcome to join us."

She sips. "Thank you, James. And I appreciate it. But no-one takes the mother-in-law on the honeymoon."

*****

Michael - Twelve Weeks

I try the switch and the bulb flicks on, then off again.
Great. The last one.
I spot Mitch, waiting at the door for me to notice her. "I was coming across to see how you're getting on. Sally asked me to give you this."

She offers me a tray bearing a pint mug of tea and one of my hotel chef's monumental 'sandwiches'. Lifting the lid, I inspect the contents; sausage, egg and bacon, tomatoes, mushrooms and brown sauce; enough protein to feed a small family for a day. And a larger family wouldn't be going hungry.

Mitch eyes the creation. "Will you eat all that?"

"Sally lives in eternal torment that I might waste away while her back is turned. I wouldn't dream of rejecting her contribution to my continued well-being."

Double-handed, I lift the thing to my mouth and bite in; a deep, delicious mouthful. "I've just gotten in the last of the wiring." Wiping a dribble of yolk from the corner of my mouth, I gesture around the room. "It's ready for you anytime you want to move in."

From ground level, Scruffy yaps, his stubby tail a dust-stirring blur. But I ignore him; I'm entitled to my breakfast.

Okay... *Second* breakfast...

He yaps again, experimentally, whines. His ears droop and trots out.

Mitch strolls around, trailing fingertips over the polished timber of the windowsill. "It's such a lovely space. Are you sure you don't want it as your office? That was your intention when you started the work..."

"I'm fine. There's plenty more still to work on." I jerk thumb to the wall. "Next door for a start."

"You're making that your work area instead?"

"Nope. It used to be a stable. It's going to be a stable again... Um..." I mumble a bit through a mouthful of bacon, then follow Mitch's horrified downward gaze.

Scruffy is back again, something dangling from his mouth. As he sees he has my attention, he drops the back-half of a rat at my feet, making a small, bloody splash on the tiles.

Oh, wonderful...

A mutt that believes in free trade...

On reflex, I stoop to pick up Scruffy's demi-rodent, then remember that I'm holding my breakfast. I can deal with a little plaster-dust in my food, but...

Sandwich still in hand, I kick the thing hard, out of the door and into some brambles. Piteous whimpering follows and I thumb a sausage downward from between the bread halves.

It's not as though I can't spare it.

The sausage vanishes in two chomps and Scruffy resumes his vigil.

Mitch follows the performance. "Where do you suppose the *other* half is?"

"I don't wish to speculate. But at least he's doing real terrier work and going after vermin. I suppose that qualifies as earning his keep."

Then, I sigh at Kirstie's pack, forming a disorderly queue by the door. Meg muscles her way in first, growling at the others. It's not as though I mind hosting the 'Gang of Four' while their mistress is still recovering from her injuries...

Ben...

...but my mid-morning 'Second Breakfast' doesn't go nearly as far as it used to.

"Meg! *Quiet!*"

The barrel-bodied little madam subsides. "Outside, the lot of you." I march them out. Archie, Mac and Emma sit, waiting expectantly. Meg grumbles as she joins them.

Taking a defiant munch of my breakfast roll, I tear off four chunks, passing them down to assorted waiting mouths then, groaning, tear off another piece as I find Scruffy has joined the end of the line, his lop-sided ears triangulating on a possible second serving. It vanishes with a *Chop!*

Returning inside with my much-reduced meal, I find Mitch, brow cocked in amusement, offering the mug of tea. "Want me to ask Sally to make you another?"

"No, I don't think I'd dare tell her most of it went to the wolf-pack." She rolls eyes outside. "How long are you keeping them?"

"Scruffy's here permanently. After Ben..." My throat tightens and I skid away from the thought. "Kirstie's four are welcome as long as it's needed. After the way she raised the alarm for you and Charlotte..."

Again, my mind veers from a subject still too painful to dwell on.

Mitch regards me for a long moment then, waving around the interior of the once-was-a-stable, "So, you're sure about me taking this? Living here? I don't want to oust you."

"Absolutely. And you're not ousting me. We'll bring across the furniture from your room in the house for the moment. You can re-furnish to your own taste as and when it suits you."

"Do you mind if I redecorate? Plain cream's pleasant enough, but..."

"Mitch, do what you want with it. Everyone needs a space to call their own. A bit of privacy. It's your home for as long as you want it. If you need anything else doing, let me know. I'm happy to do the heavy work if you'll finish off painting and whatever else it needs."

"Thank you. You don't know how much I appreciate this... Michael, how long are you happy for me to stay here? I'm sure when you bought this place, you didn't plan on having the mother-in-law move in."

"No, I didn't. It was intended to be a home for me, Charlotte and James... Which is *why* I'm offering the *mother-in-law* a space that is hers exclusively and private."

"Actually, it *is* a good idea." She blushes. "It's... It's a bit embarrassing... But last night... I could *hear* you."

Cringing at this toe-curling thought, "You're right. I'd prefer not for that to happen. Anyway..." I give her a nudge and a wink... "You might want some privacy of your own now." Her eyes widen. "Come on Mitch, a woman like you. You're a serious looker. If you want... *someone*... a man in your life... then it would be very easy..." But my words trail off at the far look in her eyes.

What's she thinking about?
*Or **who**?*
Conners?
Ex-husband. Wife-beater. Liar...
The man who let her think her little girl had been murdered...
No.
Klempner?
He said he'd leave us alone and he seems to be keeping his word.
Is she thawing out to him?
None of my damn business.

"Anyway, Mitch. This is what I've been doing for you. Let's go take a look at what you've been doing for me."

And she *smiles*.

*****

Mitch chews at a thumbnail. "Do you like it?"

I turn; around and around; taking it in. "It's... *amazing*, Mitch. I know you said you can paint, but I didn't expect this. You have a real talent."

Charlotte's mother volunteered to paint and decorate the new creche facility in the hotel. And the result is... 'Fantastic' doesn't do it justice.

At floor level, grass and flowers frame the walls; cartoon cows and sheep and horses skipping and dancing through a meadow. To one side, bulrushes and lily-pads home dragonflies, ducks and smiling frogs; all in brilliant and unlikely hues. The Amazon rain forest may have seen frogs in those colours, but certainly nowhere around here has.

Above the grass, the walls gradient from a pale pastel to the brilliant blue vault of the ceiling, the sun nesting into one corner. Golden rays finger their way through sapphire sky and white fluffy clouds. Birds swoop across the ceiling or perch on a tree towering over the lilies. Butterflies flit across the walls.

Thick green rubber matting covers the floor and boxes of toys and games are stacked into shelves, teddies and pink rabbits side-by-side with building blocks and fat wax crayons.

It is a small child's paradise.

"Mitch, it's fabulous. I can only say thank you."

The thumbnail is released, much reduced and a bit ragged. "You like it then?"

"Very much. Will you do some more for me? I'm thinking of the spa areas."

"Definitely, but... "I was *hoping* you would let me decorate the nursery for the baby." She frowns. "Have you decided on a name yet?"

"James calls the baby 'Peanut'. And until we know the baby's sex, I imagine that's as far as it will go."

"So... can I paint the nursery?"

"For myself, I'd love you to. But... this time, you'd better ask James. Let him take a look at this."

*****

James – Twelve Weeks

Wow!
 What a great job.
Mitch's work on the creche is seriously good. No-one would think she wasn't a professional.

"I based it on the room I used as Jenny's nursery when... When she was a baby... Before..." Mitch's voice catches.

I lay a hand on her arm. "You have her back now. And she's not going *anywhere*."

"I know. It's just, sometimes, when I think how I lost her..."

Her voice breaks again...

Spiralling out of control...

Change the subject...

"You have an amazing talent, Mitch. You could easily make a living as an interior decorator."

She shrinks in on herself... "Oh, I don't think so..."

Too many years of being told she has no worth?

"...Think how much time this takes. I'd have to charge the earth to make it pay."

"Alright, so you have something to sell where you *can* charge the earth." She looks askance at me, frankly unbelieving.

"Mitch, remember who your family members are. Richard and Beth move in the kind of circles where they would love something like this. 'Paying the Earth' for it would simply give them bragging value."

Her brow wrinkles, but behind her eyes, wheels are turning. "You think so?"

"I'm sure so. Take some photos of your work. Get yourself a website and you'd be good to go."

She huffs. "James, I don't know anything about the internet. I certainly don't know how to go about setting up a website."

I lay a hand on her arm. "No, but I *do*. If you want to do this, I'll get you set up with a site and show how you can do more as you're ready. And I am quite sure Charlotte would be only too pleased to help."

Her eyes flash to mine, then around the room. "You *really* think it's saleable? That I could make a living doing this?"

I fold my arms. Nod. "Yes."

She paces the room, knuckles pressed to her mouth. Then, "Do you have a camera I could borrow?"

"Only my phone, but that's not a problem. I'll ask Richard to get Marketing to send a photographer across. This will advertise you and your services. It advertises the spa and the hotel. And since, if they decide to visit, they'd at least buy a lunch in the restaurant, it even pays for itself."

"I'd... I'd not thought of it like that."

"Well, *do*. Get into that way of thinking. You have a skill, Mitch. If you learn to sell it, you're in control of your own future. Once you're earning in your own right, you'll be dependent on no-one.

*****

Klempner - Thailand

The track's a long one; a series of muddy ruts that decay to quagmire if I go any further. But it's fine. We're far enough off the main highway not to be heard.

Pulling over, I reach under the seat for the Glocks, shoving one into my belt, keeping the other in my hand. "Here's our stop, gentlemen."

Chaos in the rear...

"What's going on?"

"We're in the middle of *nowhere*."

"So, we are." I get out, then keeping them covered, unlock the rear doors. "Out you come."

Strohmayer blusters. "What the fuck's going on?" But he's sweating as he looks down the barrel of my Glock, and he's weaving on his feet.

"Delivering, as I promised, the experience of a lifetime, gentlemen. To be precise, the *last* experience of your lifetimes."

It doesn't take long. Two try to run. I take them down first. Trolley-man drops to his knees, pleading. I make it quick for him. A single round through the forehead; not even enough time to feel it.

Strohmayer seems in denial. "Do you *know* who I am?"

"Yup." I aim for his stomach, giving him a few seconds to roll around the ground, screaming in on himself as I finish the final two then, muzzle pressed to Strohmayer's temple, I say, "Don't be too sad. You're performing a valuable service to humanity today."

And I squeeze the trigger.

*****

James - Thirteen Weeks

I put the phone back into the cradle.
"All arranged?" asks Mitch from her place on the couch.
"Yes, all arranged." I rub the back of my neck. "I didn't expect to be the one *doing* this. I thought Charlotte would be telling *me*. We should have been seeing a doctor weeks ago..."
Mitch nods, looking thoughtful, then smiles as Charlotte enters.
"Ah, Charlotte," I say. "Good timing. Just to let you know, I've booked an appointment for you at a specialist pre-natal and maternity clinic..."
She stills, going 'all eyes'. "Master? What for?"
Am I hearing this?
"You're *pregnant*, Charlotte. I'd like you to have a full medical examination and..."
"I'm fine, Master. They checked me out at the hospital while I was there. Why do I need another examination?"
Mitch watches, eyes narrowing.
"I'll repeat. You're pregnant. Did you really think you wouldn't be visiting a prenatal clinic? And especially after the damage you took with that fall down the steps and everything else Ben was responsible for?"
"But, Master..."
Why is she resisting?
But I'm not accepting argument on this. "Do as you're told, Charlotte. You're *going*."
Her head hangs. "Do I have to?"
"*Yes,* you do. You chose your pregnancy. And I'm the father. That gives me a say. You're doing this."
Mitch rises from her seat, hands out-held. "Jenny, what's wrong? It's the right thing to do. And I know the reputation of the clinic James has

chosen. When I was carrying you, I could only dream of being able to call on such a place."

Face lowered, Charlotte mutters something.

I'm losing patience. "What was that?"

Still she looks down, but she speaks more loudly this time. "I don't like doctors."

Mitch laughs, patting her on the shoulder. "Tough. You're going to have to get used to them."

*****

Charlotte, flanked by me to one side, her mother to the other, scowls as we enter the clinic.

In the waiting area with us, over-made women wearing a fortune's worth of designer maternity wear and high heels...

How do you wear stilettos when you're pregnant?

... sit, drinking latte and reading glossy magazines. I pick one up while we wait, flicking through page after page of high-fashion baby clothes, which the babies are surely too young to appreciate.

Who buys this stuff?

More money than sense...

Charlotte sits, unspeaking, unresponsive.

Mitch is brisk. "Jenny, be sensible. Every pregnant woman has to see a doctor and have regular check-ups. Think of the baby."

"I *am* thinking of the baby. It's the only reason I'm here."

And I've had enough.

Hissing under my breath, *"Charlotte!* If you can't be polite to your mother, you'll regret it. Now *behave.*"

She remains sullen. "You can't punish me when I'm pregnant."

Twisting on the seat, I square her up to me by the shoulders. "You *think?* You really believe I don't have options? That I'm so uninventive or unimaginative that I couldn't think of something appropriate *if* needed?"

Mitch's mouth twitches and she looks away.

Charlotte swallows. "Sorry, Mom. I didn't mean to be rude to you."

Mitch lays a hand on her arm. "I don't understand what you have against doctors, Jenny. They're here to look after you."

But Charlotte just hangs her head.

*****

The doctor has a brisk air about her. "Good morning. Mrs Summerford? I am Doctor Redshaw. Please come this way." She turns to lead her from the waiting area.

Charlotte takes a step or two, looking over her shoulder to me and Mitch, pleading in her eye. I make to follow but the doctor holds up a hand. "Mr Summerford, I assume? I'd rather hold the consultation just with your wife to begin with."

I don't see the point in correcting her on my name. It would take too much explaining, but Mitch's eyes roll my way.

Charlotte's voice is small. "I'd *really* prefer him to come in with me. And my mother."

Why is she so nervous?

The doctor sniffs, pursing her lips. "Very well. If you really feel it necessary."

She leads us into the kind of bland white space one expects for a medical consultation room. The smell of hand-sanitiser competes with a vase of lilies on the windowsill. The walnut and leather desktop is polished to a high gleam, occupied by one of those clicking chrome executive toys and a brown manila file.

Boxes of instruments, latex gloves and syringes sit alongside shelves of heavy texts and glossy brochures from drugs and medical equipment suppliers. Posters line the wall showing various stages of development of mother and foetus. One, weirdly, asks *Have you been using contraception?*

Doctor Redshaw waves Charlotte to a seat, repeating that sniff...

Who's paying who here?

... then pulls out a couple of extra chairs for me and Mitch.

Seating herself, she flicks through the brown file, settling on a page. Looking down at the document, not at Charlotte, she traces lines of text with a manicured fingernail. "You appear to be in overall good health, Mrs Summerford. However, a few questions first. Then we can go over the test results from the examination and the scans."

Charlotte sits, all but rigid save for the winding of her fingers, knotting and re-knotting.

"I will say," continues Redshaw, "that having reviewed your medical records at some length, I would like to go over a few specific items."

Brows raised, she inclines her head, as though asking Charlotte's permission, but without waiting for a reply, continues, "First of all, I have to ask if you have continued your alcohol habit into adult life and through your pregnancy?"

Mitch's jaw drops. I think mine does too.

Charlotte comes to life. "I *do not* have an alcohol habit. I enjoy the occasional glass of wine, but I haven't *touched* alcohol since, well, since I started trying to get pregnant. And I've never been a heavy drinker."

The doctor, lips pressed flat, flicks through the file again, then taps a biro on some document. "That's not what it says here."

"What exactly *is* that file?" Charlotte's voice is a hiss. And with a sinking feeling, I know the answer.

The doctor blunders on. "It is your own medical records, from when you were in care as a child, Mrs Summerford. They are quite clear that as a teenager, you regularly drank to excess and that..."

"I did *not* drink!"

Redshaw arches a brow. "And so, how did you come to sustain a broken jaw? And..." She glances at the page again... "Also, a fractured humerus? The record states that you fell down the stairs while intoxicated. Considering that you have recently taken another fall downstairs, it is my duty to ensure that..."

Charlotte stands, white-faced. "I had a broken jaw because I was *assaulted*. I was a kid and they..." And she bursts into tears.
How did I not know this?
She's never told me...
Jade...
I jab a finger at Redshaw. "If you check the origin of that file, you will find it was produced by whatever excuse for a medic was working at the Blessingmoors home. Charlotte was a prisoner there as a child."
"Blessingmoors..." Redshaw blanches, then flips back to the cover page. "Mrs Summerford..."
But it's too late. Charlotte is stampeding out of the door, Mitch right behind her.
"You've not heard the last of this," I snarl.

*****

In the street outside, Charlotte is sobbing, Mitch with her arms around her. "Was it Larry? Did he do it to you?"
"No. It wasn't him. He never touched me. But the supervisor there..."
Mitch persists, "But Larry was in charge?"
"Yes, but he wasn't there at the time."
Bile rises in my throat. I want to hold her; to tell her that everything is alright. But I'm not sure if I should interrupt Mitch's embrace with my own. I settle for moving close, laying my hand on her shoulder. "Was it Jenkins? The man who..." And I swallow my words.
The man who died while pursuing her...
...the man she believed for years that she had killed...
The last thing she needs to be reminded of right now...
"Yes," Her sobs break loose again. "Yes, it was him. I'd escaped one time, but the police caught me and took me back to Blessingmoors, like they always did. Afterwards, Supervisor Jenkins was beating me and I

ran. He chased me up the stairs then, when he caught me, he punched me down and I fell. That's when it happened."

Mitch's voice is flat, an iced monotone. "Did you get any medical care?"

"No, they didn't realise at first what had happened, just locked me in the cellars. They only realised a few days later there was something wrong because I couldn't eat. Then they put me in the medical room and cuffed me to the bed so I couldn't run again."

The front door of the clinic opens, Doctor Redshaw appears. "Mrs Summerford, if you would just calm down..."

But Mitch gives her a look that would shrivel the skin from a peach and the woman, po-faced, retreats back inside.

Charlotte is trembling violently, her shoulder shaking under my hand. "I'm not going back in there. I'm *not*."

I meet Mitch's eyes and she passes her daughter into my arms. Holding her close, my cheek pressed to hers, I rock her, very gently, side to side. "No-one's asking you to. As for that woman, I'll be telling the manager a few home truths about bedside manner. Let's get you home..."

Where did I park?

"... Mitch, you stay here with Charlotte. I'll bring the car around."

*****

Back home, I leave Charlotte and Mitch together while I make...

Hmmm...

Comfort food...

...hot chocolate for three, topped with whipped cream and marshmallows.

Back in the lounge, Mitch is calming Charlotte, but she's still a bit weepy. Mitch herself wears a face that looks set to put the country on a war-footing.

I push the mug into Charlotte's hand. "Don't worry. I'll find another clinic for you and I'll check it out personally first; talk to the doctor myself and make sure we have someone with her brain plugged into reality."

She sniffles and won't meet my eye. "If I *have* to..."

"You do."

"... can't I go to an ordinary hospital? Where it's just ordinary people? And not..."

This isn't my Charlotte...
She's not afraid of anything...
Until now...

"Alright, I'll book us an appointment at the City Hospital, but..." I hold up a forefinger... "But if there are any complications, I reserve the right to take you to a specialist. Good enough?"

She takes a couple of breaths. "Yes, Master. Good enough."

"We're agreed then. And now..." I glance to Mitch. "You are going to tell me and your mother what happened to you when you were a child."

"I did tell you."

"Only in the briefest detail. And I'm sure you've skimmed over a lot of it. It's time to tell the full story."

*****

Nausea tugs at my stomach. I saw those cellars. I read the stories in the papers. But it's not the same as hearing it from the woman you love.

"Mitch white-faced, her features pinched "I'll never forgive him for what he did. *Never*... And to think I was beginning to..."

Klempner?
She was beginning to warm to him again?
That's busted his chances...

*****

James – Fourteen Weeks

"You and Beth should leave some of your things here; a change of clothes, toiletries. Pick one of the guest bedrooms and it's yours."

"A good idea, James." Richard strokes Beth's hair. "Are you happy with that? And it means that you and Charlotte can spend more time together while you're both expecting. Mitch too."

Charlotte's mother nods a smiling acknowledgement, but Beth positively glows...

Pregnancy suits her...

"I'd love that. Home from home. And if you're both working, we're not by ourselves."

"Perfect," I say. "That's agreed then."

Michael's face appears from around the door. "Ah, there you are."

Clothes dusty, his hair stands in plastered points and a white smear runs from nose to chin. He aims a finger at the coffeemaker. "I'll have one of those, please." Then he tosses a small brown envelope onto the tabletop by Mitch.

She picks it up, turning it over in her hand. "What's this?"

Sitting as I offer him a mug of coffee, he swings his feet up onto the table. "What I owe you for the decorating work you did on the creche."

She double-takes down to the packet. "I wasn't expecting to be paid for that, Michael. I did it to help."

His eyes crease. "I know that, but when you do work in the hotel, Mitch, you're on the payroll. I've simply paid you the same as the other decorator quoted..." He scratches at chalky hair. "... Except that's cutting you short. Your work is better than his would have been."

Mitch just stares at the packet, not opening it, but turning it over and over...

When was the last time she had money of her own?

Michael seems oblivious. "Anyway, if you let me have your bank details, I'll pay it direct next time." Forehead creasing, he regards Mitch

32

over the mug which hovers half-way to his mouth. "Is that alright? I hope there'll be a *next* time? I'd love you to do some more for me."

The packet clutched in her fingers, "I don't have a bank account."

Oh, Jeez...

Michael swings his legs down, sitting upright. "You *don't?* Why not? Oh..." his face clears. "... Was it a shared account with Frank? You're right. We'd better steer clear of that."

Still gripping the envelope, Mitch chews at a lip. "No, Frank doesn't have one either. Neither of us do. My account was closed down years ago. And then for so long, it wasn't an option because we might have been traced."

She finally releases the envelope, laying it on the table. "Then when I saw the news about Blessingmoors, when I heard Larry was in prison, I did try to open a new account, to get back into real life, but the bank wouldn't give me one."

Michael drains his mug then offers it out for a refill. "But you can't *function* in the modern world without a bank account."

"I know that, but they said I couldn't have an account without a credit record first."

Ahhh...

"And you can't get a credit record without a bank account first," I say. "Catch-22."

Her eyes raise to mine, tragedy there. Those great and glorious green eyes that I see in both her and her daughter. "That's right."

Richard has remained quiet throughout the exchange, but his gaze flicks between us as he listens in silence.

I lean over the table, propping myself on my elbows. "Does it occur to you, Mitch, that you know *just* the man; indeed, are part of his family; with the wherewithal to *lean* on a bank?"

She blinks at me, not understanding at first. Then it dawns and she turns to Richard.

His mouth puckers. "Which bank did you try, Mitch?"

"*All* of them. None would give me an account. Do you... Do you really think you could do something for me?"

He sucks in air. "I would be proud to, Mitch." At her startled glance, he simply says, "*Family.*"

Fishing in a pocket, he takes out his phone, then pauses. "Mitch, did you have any financial problems other than simply having to duck out of the system?"

She sags. "I don't truly know. I owned an apartment once, but I think it was repossessed when we ran. Certainly, I would have been listed as a defaulter. Maybe even a bankrupt. I don't know. We spent so *long* living under the radar."

Richard stares at the ceiling, a fingernail tapping at the mobile screen. After a moment, he scrolls through a couple of screens then, clearing his throat, sets the phone to loudspeaker and places it in the centre of the table.

The mobile rings three times before one of those robotically trained female voices replies. "Good morning. Gerald Hagman's secretary. How can I help you?"

"Richard Haswell here. I'd like to speak with Gerald if he has five minutes."

The voice turns off 'robot mode' and morphs to 'startled underling'. "Of course, sir. I'll see if Mr Hagman is available."

In something under fifteen seconds, the call clicks through to an artificially cheerful voice. "Richard? How *are* you? I wasn't expecting to hear from you until our lunch meeting next week. What can I do for you?"

"I have a favour to ask, Gerald. I have a friend who, through no fault of her own, is having difficulty opening a bank account. I wonder if you could oil the wheels for her. I'd take it as a personal favour."

"Of course, Richard. Of course. We'll be happy to help. Um, what is the *nature* of your friend's difficulty?"

"Some years ago, she became entangled with the wrong sorts. It resulted in the loss of her account."

A pause...

Then, cautiously, "Which bank was she with at the time?"

Richard cocks a brow at Mitch.

"City Vanguard."

The other brow arches. "Did you get that, Gerald?"

"I did, yes. Um, Vanguard collapsed... Oh... Twenty years back."

"So they did. But I am assuming that City Fidelity Credit can help my *friend* rejoin the modern age?"

Another pause... Longer this time...

"So she has no track record?"

"That's the long and short of it, yes."

"You understand, Richard, that financial institutions are tightly regulated these days..."

Richard presses a forefinger to his lips. "Of course."

"... The restrictions placed on us with the money laundering laws regarding identity and security..."

Richard's voice remains level. "She doesn't want to borrow funds, Gerald. She's not asking for credit. She simply wants a functioning cash account."

"Nonetheless, with no credit record to draw on, I'm not sure I can help you, Richard." The voice whines. "I'm terribly sorry."

Richard turns brisk. "That's fine, Gerald. Don't worry about it. I'll ask Henry Parkes when I see him at lunchtime." His eyes shift to Mitch, creasing at the corners.

Can a phone radiate silence?

It does.

Then, "You're lunching with Henry Parkes?"

"That's right." Richard grins a shark grin at Mitch, counting fingers in the air...

One... Two... Three...

... then, "Did you know he's making a pitch for the financing of F and G sites? I thought I might as well hear what he had to say. He was talking of dropping the interest rate by a couple of points if I gave him the whole deal."

Another silence.

Michael leans close to me, his voice low. "I swear the phone is icing over."

"Shhhh..."

But Richard's eyes are dancing. His fingers count another beat...

One... Two... Three... Four... Five...

"Anyway Gerald. My apologies for having interrupted you. I'll see you next week for that lunch. Give my best to Esther."

"Oh no, don't go Richard. I'm sure we can do something for your friend. Of course, rules can be interpreted..."

"*Interpreted*, yes."

"And what are viewed as regulations are often only guidelines..."

"Indeed. *Guidelines.*"

"Er... You can vouch for this person of course?"

Richard raises eyes to heaven. His voice flat once more, "Of course. You think I would ask otherwise?"

"I'll have the forms sent to your friend. Can you give me her name and address."

"Just forward them to Francis. I'll get them to her."

He taps off the phone, checks that the connection has broken, then, "Punctilious little runt. How he became CEO escapes me."

*****

In the office, Francis hands me a sheaf of paperwork. "Application forms for Mitch. Bank account application from City Fidelity."

I riffle through dozens of sheets, scanning reams of small print, written apparently in crapese, translated from burblese.

Where the fuck do they get all this rubbish from?

Richard snaps fingers at me. "James, give them to me. I'll fill them in. Mitch'll just need to sign."

Twenty-four hours and fourteen signatures later, Mitch has re-entered the modern world and holds a bank statement in her hand. The very small balance at the top of the sheet reflects her single wage payment from Michael.

He swings muddy boots up on the table...

Must break him of that habit...

"So, Mitch, you gonna do some more work in the hotel? The decor in the restaurant area's a bit boring right now."

Her eyes are glistening. "Point the way." She brandishes the statement. "But first, I am taking Jenny *shopping*."

Charlotte looks wary. "Shopping? What kind of shopping?"

Mitch's voice is triumphant. "Baby clothes!"

*****

Charlotte – Fourteen Weeks

"They're so *small*." I stare at the tiny woollen mitts my mother is showing me.

She sucks in her cheeks, but she's smiling. "Well, how big did you think Peanut will *be* when he's newly born?"

"*She*."

"You don't know that."

"I'm hoping that."

"Alright, for now, *she*. But until it's confirmed..."

None of this feels *real*.

Around me, rack upon rack of displayed baby clothes: onesies, jumpsuits, hats and caps, rompers, socks and booties...

"What *is* all of this stuff? I thought..."

My mother looks amused. "You thought what?"

"I thought, well, I'd just... *dress* her."

"In what? Irish mist? She'll need *clothes*, Jenny."

She rummages through a shelf stacked with packs of bibs, reading the labels. "Three in a pack," she mutters, then pops four packs in the cart.

"We don't need that many, surely?"

"You'll think differently when the whole lot's in the wash and she's just sicked down the last clean one." She revolves, scanning the store. "We need clothes for you too."

"Me...?"

But she's already set off; a ship in full sail, aiming for distant lands, snagging three pairs of the pink mittens and matching bootees en-route. I put two of the bib packs back on the shelf and follow her.

Taking a tee-shirt that would be a loose fit on a hippo from its hanger, she holds it against me, shoulder to waist.

"I'm never going to be *that* size."

"You think?" She sniffs, and still holding *vestment hippopotami* up to me, stands back, tilting her head and pursing her lips. "The colour doesn't suit you though."

"But I can't get to that size. You said she'll be *tiny*." I hold up the micro-mittens.

"Yes, she won't *feel* tiny when she's on the way out. And this isn't for then. It's for the next couple of months. You'll have outgrown it by then."

She takes another top from its hanger, offering the fabric to my face. "Ah, yes, a much better colour." She smiles, touching my cheek. "You having taken so much after me looks-wise, certainly makes it easier for me to find things that will suit you." She puts the tee-shirt in the basket. "Now..."

She takes a pad and pen from a pocket, ticking a couple of items off a list. "We need something fleecy for her to wear..." Her gaze reams the racks and shelves.

"Do we?"

There's a touch of impatience in her voice. "Jenny, she's due to be born in December. It's going to be *cold*. Ah..." She points her biro at a display of fluffy bunny suits. "Perfect."

Despairingly, dumping the hippopotamus shirt from the basket, I follow her.

*****

James – Fourteen Weeks

Mitch flops down on the armchair opposite mine, swiping a hand through her hair.

"Mitch, you look shattered. Haven't you enjoyed yourself? I thought you'd enjoy buying baby clothes and everything that goes with them..."

"So did I. I'm not tired. Just frustrated."

"Because...?"

"I know what's needed and I was trying to tell her, but Jenny won't *buy* anything. Take the bibs. I told her she's need a dozen at least. She bought *three*. I picked up half a dozen romper suits and she put four back." She radiates bafflement. "Is she so short of money?"

I laugh. "Charlotte's not short of money at all. She's just tight-fisted. Would you like some wine? Calm yourself down a bit."

"I'd *love* some wine."

I pour, pressing a glass into Mitch's hand, taking my own to my armchair.

Keeping my tone dry, "It's not a question of money. Charlotte has plenty of her own these days, and that's before Michael and I are involved. However..." I hold up a forefinger... "For spending on anything except books, she's as tight as a duck's arse... And..."

"And..."

I consider my words...

Do I say this?

"Charlotte's own childhood wasn't exactly enriched. She has a very narrow view of what counts as the necessities of life."

Mitch drums fingers on the chair arm. "I'd do it all myself, but I don't have that kind of money. And Jenny just doesn't seem to *believe* what's needed."

"Reality will come winging home soon enough. Look, Mitch..." I slip wallet from jacket, slipping out a credit card. "If you're happy to do it... You know what's needed and... Well, you can have fun doing all the shopping you want. I'm guessing you didn't have a lot to work with when it was your turn?"

She stares at the card. "That's true. When I was expecting Jenny, I had to make do for everything. There was no money and it was all hand-me-downs from the neighbours and second-hand stores."

"Not this time, Mitch. There's all the money you could wish for. If you think it's needed, *get* it."

She stalls. "I don't want your charity."

I huff. "Who mentioned charity? This is *me* spending for *my* daughter. But... trust me, I don't want to spend my time chasing around maternity shops. It's not my thing."

She dimples and her voice turns sultry. "James, I would *love* to spend your money on my daughter and grand-daughter."

With thumb and the tip of a forefinger she slips the card from my fingers. "I'll take her again tomorrow. And if she won't buy what's needed, I'll get it."

And with that, she sashays for the door. As she exits, she throws a glance over her shoulder. "I'm going to *enjoy* this."

*****

James - Sixteen Weeks

"Everything is looking completely normal," says the nurse, displaying a clipboard's worth of ticked boxes and scribblings. "The baby..."

Charlotte interrupts her. "Peanut..."

The nurse's mouth quirks to a smile. "*Peanut* is doing just fine. Just a trifle over the average size for the date but well within the norms. All the blood tests have the results you would hope for."

"Now..." She slides the probe over Charlotte's expanding midriff, cutting a trail through glistening gel. ""That's all looking good too." She traces a line over the screen. "You see? That's the head and you can see the heart is beating strongly."

Charlotte cranes to look. "Can you see what sex the baby is?"

"It's a bit early and the angle's off a touch with the way she's lying, but I'm pretty sure it's a girl."

Charlotte beams at me.

I stroke her fingers. "A boy would have been fine. A healthy baby is all that counts."

"I know Mast... James. But I was so *hoping* it would be a girl."

A printer clicks and whirrs.

"There you go." The tech passes me the print. "'Baby's first photo' means something different these days."

And there, in grainy black and white, is my little girl.

Your gift to me...

Jade...

Tight-throated, I tuck the photo into my wallet. "Thank you."

*****

James – Eighteen Weeks

I find Michael in the viewing gallery over the gym. "Hi. I was..."

Michael is leaning back against the wall, shaking. As he sees me, he presses a finger to his lips and thumbs towards the observation window, his eyes brimming with laughter.

As quietly as I can, I join him, keeping my voice low. "What's so funny?"

He just nods down into the gym. "*Look.*"

I follow the finger and the gaze...

Wtf?

Charlotte's in there, on a treadmill, but whereas most runners just... well.... *run*... She's....

Dancing?

"What the hell does she think she's doing?" I hiss.

Is that the Charleston?

"...You wouldn't think it was possible, would you? How the hell is she **doing** that?"

Michael is all but helpless with laughter. "Blowed if I know but trust our Charlotte. Every part a moving part, I always say, even with a bulge growing round the middle." He has *that* look in his eye.

"Can we pass over that for a minute. You don't think we should stop her?"

"Oh God, *no*. If she thought we were here, watching her, I might never get to see this again."

"She shouldn't be bouncing around like that. And what if she slips or loses her balance? She *is* pregnant. And she's already taken one fall."

He sobers up on the spot. "You're right. We'd better get in there."

*****

As we enter the gym together, Charlotte becomes a blur of movement and abruptly, is simply walking briskly on the belt. She smiles brightly. "Hi, guys."

"Hi." Michael strolls across, all casual nonchalance. "Mind if I join you?" He steps onto the next machine, walks for a few seconds, then moves up to an easy trot.

"Course not."

I talk to her reflection in the wall mirrors. "You're not over-doing it are you?"

"No. I just don't want to seize up. Or get too fat. You know, pregnant and all that."

I measure her stomach by eye. "You're right on target. And you haven't put on any excess weight. Just what's appropriate to your condition. I don't think you have anything to worry about."

"Ah-ha." She turns up her speed a notch, striding out more briskly. "Just taking precautions."

*****

Richard – Nineteen Weeks

James stretches out on a lounger close by, a tall glass and a taller jug of something colourful, floating with ice and fruit, on a side table. The beating sun might fry some of us, but his semi-Mediterranean skin seems able to handle it as he bakes to golden rather than red.

The hat over his face suggests he is dozing in the heat, but a dangling hand shifts with soft music rippling over the terrace, tapping fingers saying he is awake.

Charlotte sits on the pool edge, a light robe protecting her from the sun, dangling her feet in the water. The filmy fabric, a shade of green that complements her eyes and her pale skin, flutters in the lightest of breezes. She watches from under a floppy, broad-brimmed hat as Michael and Elizabeth frolic in the pool.

I sit down beside her, dabbling my feet too. It's pleasant under the hot sun; heated skin in the coolth of the water.

"How are you now, Charlotte? Enjoying yourself? Looking forward to the great event?" I nod down to the slight swelling of her belly where it protrudes from the filmy wrap.

Charlotte gives me a 'Princess Di' smile, looking at me from under her lashes. It's an unusual expression for her; much more something I would expect to see from my Elizabeth. Charlotte normally looks you in the eye. She may be a sub for James, but for the rest of humanity, you have to take her on her own terms.

"I'm fine."

Fine?

It's a word the entire male sex should be wary of.

Is she upset about something?

Have I upset her somehow?

Elizabeth's position as Michael's 'second wife' is settling in. The pair seem entirely relaxed with each other and both James and Charlotte seem comfortable with that.

My own position in the group is a little more ambiguous.
What am I in this?
The 'Five-Some'. This Quintet.
Or is it a Four-Some plus me?
Am I simply James' occasional sidekick?
Is Charlotte worrying about my coming close to her?
For that matter, is James?

I dart a look to my lounging friend, but his fingers still tap the beat to sixties' pop: the Monkees believe their daydreams and James taps on.

Perhaps I should have thought things through more thoroughly before I offered Elizabeth to Michael, but his depression after Ben's death... Ben's *execution*... by Klempner... seemed to make the suggestion and the timing perfectly sensible.

I watch the pair in the water. We're private here, so none of us bothers with costumes for swimming, and it's clear that the games the pair are playing not just about romping in the sunshine. He's moving ever closer to her and she's encouraging him, yelling and splashing water.

Elizabeth bursts out laughing, and Michael is on her. Whatever he's doing under the surface, she likes it.

As Charlotte and I watch, he's steering her to the edge, wrapping her fingers around the sidebar, then murmuring something soft close by her face.

Elizabeth's eyes widen, flicking to me, but I simply smile as she steadies herself against the pool wall, shoulders supported and allowing the rest of her body to float. Michael moves closer, running hands over her, thighs, breasts, the curve of her swelling stomach.

Charlotte leaning back on her hands, smiles too, from under her hat.

Yes, she's perfectly happy with them...
What then?

Charlotte, a few weeks further into her pregnancy, is somewhat larger than Elizabeth, not that it's obvious under the loose sun-robe.

"How are you feeling now? Still getting the nausea at all?"

"No, that's gone now." She smiles, but the smile is wistful. "I've not felt any sickness for at least a month now."

So, something else is upsetting you?

Is it me?

Take the bull by the horns.

"Charlotte, is something bothering you? Is it me? Have I done something to annoy you?"

Her glance jolts my way. "Oh, no. No, not at all. It's great having you..." She stumbles on her words, then sweeps a look by James, then Michael. "... having you as part of *us*."

And now she smiles properly at me, with that *alike-but-not-alike* smile that I know from my own Elizabeth, but which in Charlotte, is uniquely *hers*.

From the pool, Elizabeth squeals.

Inside, I grow warm. I take her hand, kiss the fingers. "Something *is* bothering you, Charlotte. What is it? Can I help?"

She flushes. "I... I wanted to get pregnant. To have the baby..." Her gaze flashes to James, still under his hat. "It's just... It would be nice if I could be pregnant without getting so fat."

And I burst out laughing.

"Oh, Charlotte. You're *not* fat. You're the size you should be." I pat her stomach. "And you'd better get used to the idea that you're going to get a lot larger than this."

"I know." Her voice falls and she looks down at her dangling toes, swishing them through the water.

"Charlotte?"

She isn't vain. The primping and preening so many women devote so much time to, has never been her style. Most of the time she seems perfectly content with jeans, tee-shirts and her hair in a plain ponytail.

And I have seen for myself that James' occasional attempts to spend money on her for clothes seem to fall into some abyss.

But that's when she takes her good looks for granted...

Now...

"Charlotte, you're not worrying about your appearance, are you? Trust me, you look wonderful."

Spots of red pinch at her cheeks. "I feel so fat and clumsy. I try to walk past things and keep bumping into them, 'cos there's more of me than I think there is. And it's in different places. And if I stand up for too long, I get tired. And..." Her voice rasps, "And I need to *pee* all the time."

The Monkees have stopped believing and instead, Dionne Warwick is walking by, but James' hand has stopped tapping.

"Charlotte, you surely can't believe that because you're pregnant, somehow, you're suddenly unattractive?"

She says nothing, face low, sucking at her lips.

Laying a palm on either shoulder, I twist her to face me. "Charlotte..." Her head hangs and she's gulping. "Charlotte, *look* at me when I speak to you."

Her faces rises a little and I tip up her chin to help it the rest of the way.

"Sir?"

"Charlotte, you and that lovely woman over there..." I jab a finger towards the pool... "Yes, *that* one. The red-haired water-nymph with the handsome blond man working his way between her thighs... The pair of you are the most beautiful women I have ever known. Being pregnant is irrelevant. Men would lie at your feet if you let them."

"Really?" Her voice has a rushy undertone.

"Yes, *really*. Both of you, you and Elizabeth."

She smiles a little, sighs and looks out to sea. Gulls swoop, haunting the blue with their cries. A slight breeze ripples dancing water.

"It's a magical place this, isn't it," she says.

"It is indeed."
Is this a change of subject?
I'm not sure.
She looks up and down the beach. "You're very lucky, having something like this; the beach house."

"Very little luck in it. I bought the land and built the house myself, so I had just what I wanted."

Her mouth makes a little 'O' of surprise. "I'm surprised you got permission to build it here."

I rub the side of my nose. "Being wealthy has its advantages. There *was* a *quid pro quo*, but on that basis, I got my beach house."

Humour twitches at her lips. "What was the *pro quo*?"

"The mayor wanted to build an extension to the university campus in the City. After he argued me down for a while, I agreed."

She eyes me, raising a brow.
No fooling you…

I lean in. "The truth is, I'd planned to do it anyway, as part of the City renovation project, but of course, he didn't know that."

She bursts out laughing, then turns sober again. "It was here you know, that first summer when you let us stay here, that the three of us first really became *Three*: our Triad."

"*Let* you stay?" Pulling on my chin, I chuckle. "In truth, it was more of a bribe to keep James on hand when I was in a tight spot."

She arches her brows, looking over her shoulder to where James lies under his hat, quite still.

Too still.

"He never told me that."

"Perhaps he never realised himself how *much* of a bribe it was."

James doesn't move.

"Whatever the reason, it made us. The three of us." She looks to her Master again, then to where her Lover, still frolics with Elizabeth in the pool.

My gaze drifts to the blond man, currently 'servicing' my giggling wife.

"Enjoying that, Beth?" he says. "Want more?"

Her head lolling back, eyes squeezed closed, "Oh, God, yes."

His hands under her hips, she's supported by the water too. Her legs are wrapped tightly around his waist, her arms around his neck and, his face buried in the crook of her neck, Michael slow-fucks her. Elizabeth's face, then eyes, rise to meet mine over his shoulder, her face pink with sexual heat, green eyes bright in the sunshine.

My cock twitches.

Charlotte watches them for a few moments. "We had some ups-and-downs, but we came out of that summer as our 'Triad'."

"And what are we now? I nod towards the pair.

Her brow creases. "How do you mean? *What are we?*"

"You *were* a Triad. Now Michael has Elizabeth. Soon both you and she will have your first child. The first offspring of our... Our *what?* Our family? Are we a single family now?"

She turns to me, a hand to her forehead against the sun, forehead crinkling. "Richard, what are you asking me? We've always been family. Ever since that first time you saw my birth certificate and knew that Beth and I are related."

"So... is that how you think of me? A kind of brother in law?"

"*Aaahhh...*" She lets out air, staring vacantly out over the sea.

James voice rumbles from under the hat. "Richard asked you a question, Charlotte. Are you going to reply? Or do I come and school you in good manners?"

Her gaze slanting his way... "Um, yes, Master. I'll answer."

"Go on then."

Her gaze turns vacant again. "No, I don't think of you as a brother-in-law. Not now. I did at first, but not now."

"So... *now*...?"

James stirs, replacing the hat with mirrored sunglasses as he sits up on his lounger, arms loosely locked around his knees and now clearly listening in.

Charlotte swings back, looking around to him. But he doesn't speak, simply tilting his head. Behind the sunglasses, it's hard to read his expression, but his lips curve.

She swings her legs from the water to lie back, stretching out on her towel. She looks to me, then to James and back to me. Her eyes locked with mine, arms stretched out over her head, she raises her knees, a little akimbo.

My cock jerks and my balls heat.

The thin wrap hides nothing: the convex mound of her belly, the rise of her breasts - always large but now, with her advancing pregnancy, even more so.

James...

Do I ask his permission?

He watches, eyes hidden behind the blue-green reflection of his lenses, but doesn't react.

I glide my hand over her. Warm flesh, firm but yielding, and now her rising perfume: the scent of desire and sex.

From the water, Elizabeth is watching. Over Michael's shoulder her jewelled eyes follow my hand as I stroke Charlotte. Slipping a hand between her knees, I ease her a little further open. In the pool, lower down as she is, Elizabeth shifts and cranes, trying to see what I am doing, Michael becoming aware that something is happening behind him.

He turns, bringing her with him then, when he sees us, disentangles Elizabeth from his waist and neck, rolling her to float belly down in the water, hitching her hands onto the sidebar. Then scissoring in between her legs again, he re-enters her, now with both of them facing us.

"Beth..." Michael slightly disengages from her for a moment, stepping back. His voice is low but clear, intended to be heard by all.

"What would you like? Tell me." He moves in the water, to float a little over her.

Elizabeth's eyes flick between Michael and me, then to Charlotte, to James and back again. James straightens up, his head tilting. Charlotte also sits up, her grin morphing from enthusiasm to cheek.

"I..." Elizabeth begins, then stutters to a halt.

Michael stands between her splayed legs, holding her with a hand at each knee and buried inside her, "Yes? Beth...? C'mon, talk to me. What do you want?"

"I..." She colours up. Gulps...

Shaking his head slightly, nonetheless, from his place behind her, the blond man is smiling. "Beth, if you knew nothing else about me, surely you must realise that there's nothing you could want to ask that is going to offend me. *What* would you like?"

Her voice is quiet yet, somehow, carries. "I'd like to watch."

"Okay. Sure." He withdraws, then pulls her upright to stand in the water facing him. "Watch *what?*"

Her eyes dart to Charlotte, then to me and she bites her lip.

Michael's gaze follows hers. "You want to watch Richard on Charlotte?"

She nods, slowly. "Yes... But..." And she stops, looking to James. He sits up straighter, sucking in his cheeks, lips twitching.

"Yes..."

She's still holding back...

Behind Michael's face, the penny drops. "Me too? You want to see the three of us on Charlotte?"

Elizabeth bites at that bottom lip, eyes wide, flushed, slowly nodding.

James sweeps off his sunglasses, no smile on his lips. But nonetheless, it lurks at the corners of his eyes. "Have you considered keeping your sub in order, Richard?"

My voice bland, poker-faced, "It's so hard to find the good ones these days."

Michael's eyes dart between me, James and Charlotte. "Y'know, Beth, you're breaking new ground here. We've never been in a four-way. Charlotte... How do *you* feel about that?"

She grins.

How many has she handled at once? When James first had her... A lot more than three...

My groin jolts and my cock rises.

*****

Charlotte – Nineteen Weeks

Michael pulls himself, naked, up from the pool, shivering off water. Then turning, he offers Beth a hand, pulling her up and out. He's already hard, his erection flagging a little from the coolness of the water but firming up again in the warm air.

Pulling out a seat from the table, he arranges it under the shade of the umbrella, then turns to Beth, offering her a light robe. "Make yourself comfortable. Don't catch the sun."

Richard, looks to her, speaking with mock severity. "You've come on a long way since the day Michael first agreed to be your 'Birthday Present'. You ask *him* for something like that, but not me?"

Beth blinks. "It's different with you, Master."

I'm not sure Richard is pleased by her answer. "*How?* How is it different?"

My Master rises from his seat with a smooth grace, standing over me, looking down. Straight-faced, nonetheless, his dark eyes crinkle at the corners. "Richard, you're Beth's Dom. Michael is her Lover. Just as it is between Michael, Charlotte and myself. It's a different relationship."

Richard inhales, stretching up, hands clasped behind his neck, looking up at the sky.

Does he get that?

Then he chuckles, scratching the side of his nose. "So, Charlotte, what do you think? Two out-and-out Doms *and* your Lover?"

Before I can answer, my Master breaks in. "Charlotte, are you ready to oblige your cousin? Beth would like a show."

Arousal thrills through me. My Master already bulges in his trunks. Richard too. Noticeably, he shares my Master's expression of apparent severity. I'm not fooled. They're both enjoying this.

Michael is well ahead of them, his erection already at full mast. I know that there were times, when we first knew each other, that he was reluctant to 'share' me. Apparently, Richard is an exception to this.

My Master says, "Why don't you lie down Michael." He gestures to the lounger. "I think we can start off with Charlotte straddling you and take it from there."

Michael, his grin very white in the sunshine, lies down, arranging himself, cock ahoy. Richard and my Master each offer me a hand, pulling me to my feet, then my Master grips me from behind by the shoulders. "Richard, would you care to undress Charlotte?"

"My pleasure."

His voice is soft, but as he squares up to me, I see the 'Dom' take over. My 'undressing', such as it is, consists of Richard seizing the hem of my robe and lifting it up and away.

Then he stands back, travelling me with his eyes as my Master slips hands from my shoulders and down. One palm cups the swelling of my belly. The other glides further south, winding through the curls at the vee of my thighs, then dipping in. His face close by mine, the indrawing of his breath is loud, the exhalation warm on my cheek.

"Warm and wet and as ready as ever," he murmurs. He kisses my cheek then, "I believe you know what is expected of you now, Charlotte." A palm between my shoulder blades, he gives me a gentle shove towards Michael.

Three of them...

All together...

My insides liquefying, already the heat rises in my face.

From his position flat out on the lounger, Michael's smile grows broader as he offers out a hand. "You coming on board, Babe?"

And as I swing a leg over the lounger and Michael's flag-pole groin, from behind, hands steady me...

... Four hands, holding me at shoulders and waist, fingers gripping in until, poised over Michael, his erection eased against my warming entrance, I lower myself, taking him inside me.

Stretching me...

Gradually filling me...

My Lover...

My Husband...

It's so *sweet*...

Electricity pulses up through my core, taking my flesh with it. All of itself, my pussy tightens and clutches around him.

The hands behind me shift. To my left, one hand settles to cup a breast, another to tweak at the nipple. To my right, fingers comb through my hair, massaging my scalp then drawing my hair together into a tight handful.

Beth sits, watching, lips parted, her breathing rapid and shallow. Through the thin shift, her breasts rise and fall, her face is sheened and her eyes are wide and brilliant. Green irises war with huge black pupils.

From behind me, Richard's voice: "Elizabeth, play with yourself. Let us see you. And turn so that Michael can see you too."

At his words, inside me, Michael's shaft, already huge, twitches and swells even further. Gripping me, both hands at the hips, he lifts me a little, an inch or two, holding me steady as, first gently, then more strongly, he thrusts up.

The hand gripping my hair twists. "Richard wants to see his cock in your mouth Charlotte. So does Beth. Open wide."

Even if I wanted to resist, I couldn't. Slowly, inexorably, my head is steered around.

From behind me the sound of rustling fabric then, Richard, naked, erect, moves to face me, stooping to softly kiss me.

Then thumbing over my lips, he pushes inwards, pushing past my teeth. "Open up, Charlotte." Easing his thumb inside. "Wider."

He stands for a long moment, looking down at me, his thumb pressed into my mouth.

I have that odd feeling I get at these moments:

My Master, dark-eyed, dark-haired, severe. Michael, blond, blue-eyed, so beautiful...

Richard is dark-haired but blue-eyed and with that touch of steel that adds to his air of power. I'm not sure if he knows that himself, but it is so ingrained that it is *simply* a part of him.

And I'm sure Beth recognises it too; something of what drew her to him at the beginning and which holds her now.

He presses down on my jaw with the thumb, widening my gape. "That's good."

Then he withdraws it, instead moving closer to offer me his seeping erection, wiping salty tangy pre-cum over my lips. "Lick it away, Charlotte."

But I don't need telling, lapping at the briny treat, first from my lips then from the oozing slit of his shaft where a dewdrop, a bright bead in the sunshine, trembles on the purplish head.

I want to take him in, to suck and lick at this delicious cock-sicle, but rocked by Michael's pumping, I can't hold steady. As I bob up and down, Richard's erection escapes me. I reach again, mouth wide and this time, Richard pushes forward and in, anchoring himself on my mouth.

My Master's hands leave me briefly. Again; the rustle of fabric; then I am grasped once more. Pulling me firmly back by the shoulders, he props me with his body, steadying me, the press of his erection against my spine, sandwiched between my body and his, my sweat and his pre-cum lubricating his movement.

Curving a hand around, he plants a palm on my chest. The other knots into my hair, restraining me further, and sweet arousal spikes through me to where Michael thrusts up from below, and my cunt pulsates and clutches at him while Richard works himself into my mouth, a steady salt-sweet trickle as he face-fucks me.

I feel rather than hear my Master's groan, vibrating through my ribs as his cock is repeatedly squeezed and released by the movement of my body. A low, quaking rumble, it echoes through bone and flesh, like thunder down to my core and spiking arousal to my clit.

Blood pounds in my skull, drumming behind my ear and, through squeezed lids, sending light and dark kaleidoscoping behind my eyes.

From offside, another groan, a female sound, and I flicker lids open again.

Beth: she's fucking herself, fingers gleaming as she dips in deep, then out again to rub at her bud.

Michael flicks eyes across to her, his hips still undulating under me: an easy flowing motion, his cock in and out... in and out...

His eyes, so blue against his tan, hold her for a few moments before, looking up again, he smiles. He releases one of my hips briefly to stroke to my face. "Okay, Babe?"

Heat flushing up my neck and cheeks, I break free of Richards's streaming erection just long enough for a muffled, "*Mmmmff,* yes," before he claims my mouth again.

His grin relaxes to a smile then, gliding the hand down, he smooths over a breast, tilting his head as he does so. His pupils are wide and black against a rim of blue as, cupping my breast, he thumbs at a nipple.

Then the hand slides south again to stroke over my belly, and back to the hip, supporting me once more as he *lunges* upwards.

Beth, her face and breasts and swollen belly aflame, thighs and fingers shiny, fixes her eyes on mine as she works herself, plunging fingers deep into the vee of her thighs... Then her gaze goes opaque and she whimpers, her head falling forward as she fucks herself through orgasm.

Richard, so close to me, shudders, looking alternately between his climaxing wife and his erection in my mouth. The soft musk of his groin and the sweet tang of his flow over my tongue send my arousal spiralling upwards to climax: a whirling tornado, that as I shift my gaze upwards, is reflected in his eyes. The heat I see there warms me more than the sunshine, passion simmering.

He bucks, head dropping forward. "*Fuck,* Charlotte." His voice rasps as, abruptly, he pulls clear and spurts, splashing over my face.

He pulses; once, twice, thrice, his cum trickling over down over my skin then, wiping my face with a palm, he stoops to open his mouth over mine.

What passes between us? I don't have a name for it. But as the smile unfolds from his eyes, his kiss is hot and dark and deep, and after a moment, my Master relinquishes his hold on my hair, releasing me to him.

Under me, Michael grunts, his fingers sinking into my flesh. His head presses back and his mouth flings wide... "Christ..."

Behind me, my Master's shaft rubs against my spine: firm, yet yielding; hard but smooth, as he slides higher then lower, and up against me, slick and warm as he works himself against me...

And higher, his chest pressed against my shoulders, the thump of his heartbeat quickens, thundering against my body: faster, harder...

More...

He stiffens, groaning, and wet heat splashes behind me.

And that's enough: the Rush takes me, my own flesh pulsating, my sight going blind, my awareness turning inside as wave after pleasurable wave ripples through my sex and my thighs, making heart and head pound. Even the tips of my fingers tingle...

Until, sated, my pussy hums to a stop, purring in satisfaction.

God, but that was good...

My Master presses against me; his hard body to my spine, his face to the crook of my neck and shoulder, his breathing deep, heavy, gradually easing...

Richard looks to Beth, turns briefly to me, caressing my face, then returns to his wife. Arms outstretched, "My Love..."

I drop to my hands, and a grinning, though softening, Michael reaches for my swinging tits with his mouth and hands

His voice is muffled. "Thank you very much..."

Stars behind my eyes, my heartbeat pounds downhill, slowing bit by bit. Getting my breathing back to a handleable level, I unhitch from

Michael and then, with a bit of help from my Master, lower myself onto the next lounger.

Michael hauls himself upright. "I think that calls for cold drinks all round." And tugging on a pair of shorts, he vanishes inside.

I lie back, still descending from the heavens. "Oh, that was *great*. But it's going to wear me to a sliver."

My Master eyes me slant-wise, his mouth twitching. "So, you're not enjoying having *three* husbands?"

There's a twinkle in his eye, but the question sobers me. "Is that really what's happening? I know we talked... Michael and Beth... but..."

My Master, my *husband de facto*, sits by me, stroking my hand. "I'd say that is what is happening, yes. The reality of the situation." His brow creases. "Does that bother you?"

Does it?

"It seems terribly... *greedy*... of me to have three husbands."

"Why?" He swings an arm, gesturing to Richard and Beth, locked in a close embrace, murmuring to each other. "You have always liked and respected Richard..." Richard notices, nodding but returns his attention to Beth. "... And you were attracted to him the moment you met."

And on that, I'm still uncertain of what to say.

My Master pauses, then seems to feel the need to fill the silence. "None of us will be left bereft. Lost. Abandoned. Whatever children our group produces will be protected, loved... *cherished*.... Alright, so the first child is, biologically speaking, yours and mine. The second will be Beth's and Richard's. And you have promised the next to Michael. But the biological relationships are beside the point. Children need a loving family. *Ours* will always have that. So long as they are nurtured and raised by adults who love them, what does the exact parentage matter?"

"I'm... never sure what to make of Richard."

My Master tilts his head, brow wrinkling. "In what way?"

"How he feels about me... No... What he *thinks* of me. I mean... he... seems attracted to me, but he loves Beth so much. I don't know..."

My Master shrugs. "You could say the same for Michael. He loves you deeply, but nonetheless is also attracted to Beth. I would say it is both the similarities and the contrasts between the pair of you that is the attraction. Physically so alike. Emotionally so unalike. And..." He mulls for a moment... "I suspect it is the same for Richard. In his case he is um..." He rocks his hand back and forth... "He is coming from the *other end*, as it were." His lips twitch again.

Devilment stirs in me. "And you, Master?"

He leans close, slipping his hand behind my head and looping my ponytail into his fingers. Steering my face to his, "I am *yours*. And I have been since the days I saw a pair of green eyes in an auction catalogue."

And his mouth falls over mine.

*****

Michael – Twenty Weeks

I'm enjoying the view. Looking over the sea, the sand and the dunes is pretty good. Watching Beth and Charlotte sitting together exchanging pregnancy notes and gossip is even better.

Then the peace is broken...

Raised voices...

No... not exactly *raised*... but determined... Angry even...

And without a hint that either party intends to back down.

Who is it?

I cock an ear...

James and... *Ross??*

*What on **earth** would they be arguing about?*

The girls both turn, Charlotte's eyes wary, Beth's worried.

Putting my drink down, "I'll see what's happening. You two stay here."

I follow the palaver back inside, meeting Richard en-route, who looks as baffled as I feel. "What the hell would those two argue about?"

"Not a clue. We'd better see what's going on."

And together we track the racket to the kitchen where James and Ross are manoeuvring for position around the table like a pair of bull elephants with toothache.

Ross slams an onion down onto a chopping board. "*I* cook for Mr and Mrs Haswell."

James brandishes a cheese grater like Zues threatening the impious with thunder-bolts. "*I've* been cooking for them for months, whenever they've visited my home."

"Exactly. Your home, *Mr* Alexanders. *Your* home. This is Mr Haswell's property..."

"But *this* dinner is for extra guests. And I invited them..."

"Give me strength..." I mutter.

Next to me, Richard grunts agreement.

James slaps a garlic bulb onto his own chopping board, then comes down on it hard with the flat of a knife. The bulb shatters, cloves shoot off in all directions and I duck smartly to avoid the shrapnel.

Richard thunders in. "Oh, give it a rest, the pair of you." They freeze. "*James,* you do the starter and the dessert. *Ross,* you do the main. That way we all get a bit of peace and quiet."

The wisdom of Solomon...

"But..."

"I was just..."

"That's the *end* of it. As you both just agreed, my house. So, it's my rules."

*****

I look over the place settings. "Seven? So, who's the company we're expecting?"

James sets napkins by each place, still chuntering under his breath. "We're celebrating Kirstie leaving hospital. I invited her and Ryan along. Help them get back into the social scene again."

"Great idea. Do we know if they're actually a couple again?"

James straightens up. "Not sure. The last I saw she still wasn't wearing his collar. But I think some normal interaction with friends may help smooth that one along."

"*You* are playing matchmaker?"

"*Yes,* I am. I *like* Kirstie. She's been a good friend. More than a friend, considering what she's suffered. And... I've not forgotten that I fucked things up when she first asked me to help her with Ryan."

"That wasn't your fault. Ryan was being a pig-headed moron, not accepting what it takes to be someone's Dom."

"Well, maybe. Maybe not. I still feel responsible."

*****

The sound of a car outside. Scruffy barks, running in excited circles by the door, his runty tail a-quiver.

Richard eyes him, sucking in his cheeks. "You know, if this house was ever going to host a dog, I'd have envisaged something rather more elegant than that. A setter perhaps, or maybe a deerhound. Something with a bit of style and aristocracy."

"You mean you didn't want something that looks like it was built from the bits all the other dogs didn't want?"

He gives me a dry look then make his way down the hall to the door. Somewhere along the route he paints on his best 'Host' face.

"Kirstie. Ryan. Do come in, the pair of you."

Kirstie, tall and elegant as ever, not pretty, not exactly beautiful either, but striking with her strong features and aquiline nose. In a loose summer dress, her dark hair long and free, she's linked arm in arm with Ryan and with just a hint of leaning on him for support.

But her long swan neck is bare of ornament.

I shake hands with Ryan then lean close to kiss Kirstie on the cheek. "Wonderful to see you back on your feet, Kirstie."

*****

The meal is *exquisite*. The first course, French onion soup, arrives hot and fragrant straight from the oven. The cheese crust, bubbling and golden, floats atop a dark broth which is somehow savoury and sweet at the same time.

"Great soup," says Kirstie.

James beams. "Glad you think so."

The main course is rack of lamb. Crisp and succulent, there's rosemary and... I chew, analysing the flavour... Normally I would simply ask James, but not today...

Charlotte pipes up to Ross, standing in the wings as waiter. "Lovely roast, Ross. What's that fruity flavour?"

"It's plum and clove, Mrs Summerford. I basted the lamb with preserve made from the fruit I picked in Mr and Mrs Haswell's garden last year."

She smacks her lips, marking out her words with an upraised fork. "It's *really* good. Michael, I'll have to plant some fruit trees in our garden too. Sally would love that for the restaurant kitchen."

Thunder rolls over James' face.

I bite into another succulent mouthful. "Great idea, eh James?"

Ross smirks, pointedly looking anywhere but at James.

Kirstie leans in, her head close to mine. "What's going on?"

"Don't worry about it. Just James and Ross indulging in a little edge play."

"Ah..." She hides a smile behind a glass of cava. "Oh, by the way, Charlotte. Did that doctor find you?"

Charlotte looks blank. "Doctor? What doctor?"

"Um, Ramora, I think he said. Yes, Doctor Ramora. He came by last week asking after you, just before I was signed out for the last time. I told him you'd moved out weeks ago."

"Ramora?" Charlotte swings her head. "Doesn't mean a thing to me. What did he look like?"

"Tallish, heavily built. Looked more like a bouncer then a doctor actually."

Charlotte laughs. "Doesn't ring a bell. Maybe he was looking for my records and they'd got the departments mixed up." She shrugs, dismissing it.

*****

"So... Charlotte... What's in the future for your mother?" asks Ryan. "Happily single? Or is she looking for a man in her life?"

Charlotte chews slowly. "I don't think so. I think she's enjoying taking control of her own life again. She spent so long, so many years, having *no* control... Events spinning around her. One man or another telling her what she *had* to do, or manipulating her into it... Whether she liked it or not... Stephen, my father, Frank..."

Ryan pushes food around his plate. "It's about understanding the limits isn't it," he says after a while. "About what's agreed between people. What is consented to. 'No' means 'No'. Would you agree, James?"

James' expression is solemn, but his words are smooth. "I *would* agree, yes. 'No' *does* mean 'No'."

"Yes... consent is the key to the bond between a couple..." Ryan appears to be replying to James, but his eyes are on Kirstie.

"Yes," she whispers. "Consent is the key." And a smile whispers over her lips.

*****

Dessert when it arrives, is a fairyland confection of fruit and spun sugar with enough whipped cream to lay a ski slope.

Ryan huffs and leans back, abandoning his spoon to hold his middle. "Absolutely delicious. Superb."

"There's plenty more," says James.

"Couldn't eat another thing. You've surpassed yourself, James." He twists around. "You too, Ross. Amazing."

Kirstie dabs at her mouth with a napkin. "Yes, I'd no idea that testosterone is such a well-developed flavour."

Richard explodes into a fit of coughing. After a few seconds, he straightens up again, wiping at his eyes. "Sorry about that. Bone got stuck in my throat."

James picks a morsel of fruit from between his teeth with a fingernail. "Yes, do watch out for bones everyone. You can't be too careful with rhubarb." But there's a twinkle in his eyes for Kirstie.

"That was great." Charlotte stands, "But sorry, I gotta pee."

*****

You're staying overnight I hope? says Richard.

Well... Kirstie sucks at her lips, then looks down. Ryan looks away.

"There's plenty of room," says Beth. "We have several spare bedrooms and I had them all made up in case we had extra visitors..."

Are they sleeping together?

"... So you can choose where you would like to sleep." She waves a vague hand upwards. "The Green room, that's a twin, has a stunning view in the morning. It's angled so you get the dawn over the dunes. It's my favourite when I'm here without Richard."

Richard blinks. "You don't sleep in our bed when I'm not here?

"No, my Love. When you're not with me, I have other things in my life. "

He blinks some more, shifting in his seat, then forehead creasing, takes a sip of his brandy.

*****

James murmurs, "Well, will you look at *that*..."

"What?"

He pulls the curtain back, pressing a finger to his lips and nodding out.

In the background, soft music is playing, drifting through open windows out to the soft, slow, summer evening over the terrace and beach. And there, out by the strandline, are Kirstie and Ryan.

He's sitting on the sand, knees tucked up into his arms, barely smiling but his eyes locked on her as she dances for him

She's a tall girl, lithe and lean. Her long dark hair emphasises her height, and rippling in the wind as she moves, her grace too. She sways and shimmies with the music, her loose dress fluttering in the slight breeze, shifting with her motion.

As the track finishes, she stills, outstretches a hand, an invitation.

His head tilts back, his mouth opening a little, then their hands meet as she draws him up off the sands.

He hesitates, but as she gazes him full in the face, he moves closer, then an arm around her waist, pulls her in tight.

"Think they're going to get back together?"

"It's looking promising isn't it. It would be a shame if they didn't. They make a good couple."

"They do. Let's get that mood going for them again."

Turning off the light so as not to be backlit, I hover over my choice...

Music to dance by...

Music to dance *together* by...

Unchained Melody... Perhaps the most beautiful song ever written for lovers.

As the new piece starts, Kirstie moves again, swaying to the rhythm, now in Ryan's arms. And as the wistful tones of the Righteous Brothers drift over the sands, the two dance together, body to body, cheek to cheek.

"Ah, that's lovely..."

I jolt back to reality. I'd not heard Charlotte enter.

"... I do hope they'll get back together."

*****

In the deep of the night, I rouse, blinking into darkness. Charlotte rests her face on my chest. James is spooned up behind her.

What woke me?

And there, from somewhere in the darkness... muted but unmistakable, the cry of a woman in climax.

I listen and the sound cuts off short, but I roll back to sleep with a smile.

*****

Over the clatter of breakfast plates, the sound of a door opening. Kirstie and Ryan, hand-in-hand, and very obviously *together.*

And at her throat, from a fine velvet choker, dangles a pearl.

Kirstie's eyes meet mine for a moment. She smiles and with an all but imperceptible movement, she nods.

Good morning. I hope you slept well?

Assuming they slept at all.

*****

Klempner - Thailand

Is that him?

Pushing the spectacles up my nose, across the dining room, I survey the entrance lobby and the group just entering. Three men, all Hispanic types plus a blowsy-looking female cramming a size-sixteen body into a size-twelve dress.

No. He'd never be with a woman looking like that.

The hotel is classy-looking, expensive. It should be considering what I paid.

Air-con whispers over the assembled diners. They murmur, telling themselves they're enjoying the high life as they eat over-priced meals. The food's good but considering some of the slums not so far away, and the money some of the locals get by on, the prices are offensive.

Odd... There was a time that wouldn't have occurred to me...

I sit reading my tablet, propped up by a jug of oil and another of chilli sauce. Occasionally, I fork up prawns and rice in a vivid green sauce. Fragrant with garlic, limes and cilantro, it should be stirring my appetite, but my attention is elsewhere.

This beard is driving me *nuts...*

... But I resist the urge to scratch. It wouldn't fit with the persona. While I have to meld with the bourgeoisie at play, I need to maintain the front.

If I have it right, all anyone else will see is a prosperous businessman: well-groomed, the suit casual but expensively cut, in a pale linen which suits the climate and merges nicely with the others around me. I see occasional glances, weighing up the cut, the cost and perhaps the tailor, but that's perfectly normal for this crowd where everything is measured by your wealth...

... apparent wealth at any rate...

But the moment I have the chance, the beard's coming *off.*

Thank God for air-con...

So, I ignore the infernal itching, trying to lose myself in my research.
How did we manage before the internet?
And satellite mapping?
My table-companion picks at her food. She's young, blond and sultry-eyed, and beautiful in an obvious, off-the-conveyor-belt kind of way. She would win many a *Miss-Beauty-Contest* competition and practices a pout she imagines is attractive.

She keeps trying to catch my eye, pushing bok choy around her plate. "Can we talk about something?"
Don't strain your brain...
Could I manage without her?
No... A single man would be noticed.
My eyes fixed on my screen. "You're not being paid to talk."

"Oh." Subdued, she turns what passes for her attention back to her meal. "I just wondered, why I'm here. You don't seem very..."

"You're here because I'm *paying* you. I'm asking very little for what you're earning. Now, eat your meal and try to look as though you're *enjoying* yourself."

She shuts up, and I take the opportunity to scan outwards...
Any sign of him?
...looking through to the glass screens to the hotel entrance, and beyond; the frontage out to swimming pools, manicured lawns and the beach.
No, not yet...
I scroll through satellite images, searching for my target...
There you are...
The detail's pretty good.
Now, how to get there...
And get out again...
The routes through the local forests are varied, not all of them are easy and some are close to impossible.

It penetrates that Airhead's talking again, wittering on...

Her eyes on her plate. "...I mean... It's been four days now. And I'm bored with sitting by pools and bars and... Can't we go out somewhere?" She straightens up, breathing in, giving me the benefit of her cleavage.

"*No.* You can do whatever you want, just so long as it's done quietly and *here.*"

"But I'm so *bored.*"

"So read your magazine."

"I've read it."

"There's plenty in the lobby, written in English."

"Reading's boring."

Only boring people get bored...

My eyes rise briefly to hers and then down again to my tablet.

Give me strength...

"Can I go for a swim?"

"Later."

"Can I have another cocktail?"

For fuck's sake, shut up...

"Order whatever you want."

A waiter appears by some magic over her shoulder. "Yes, madam?"

"I'd like a cocktail, something local... Um..."

I scissor in on an opening in the forest canopy. "Try a Siam Mary."

Is that a trail?

It's not on the tourist maps...

Something like curiosity piques her tone. "What's that?"

"Like a Bloody Mary, but regional ingredients."

She squeaks up to the waiter, "I'll have one of those."

"And for you, sir?"

"I'll have a sparkling water: ice and lime. Room number 317. Name of Plumber."

There's movement by the entrance.

Keeping my face fixed on my tablet, I look from under my brows to the two dark-suited men entering the hotel. Big bruisers, with the kinds of faces only a mother could love and with a manner that says they get all their 'authority' from someone else. Obvious heavies.

Ah-haaaa...

Shifting in my seat, I shift to watch... directly to the door... from over my tablet

Bullying their way through the bustling holiday makers, the two clear the way for the man behind them.

Garcias...

He strolls in; his loose linen jacket immaculate despite the heat and the humidity. A woman accompanies him, strolling with a swing to her hips. Tall, blonde, elegant, beautiful. She reeks of money, designer clothes and the kind of education that teaches a woman how to *behave*. But there's no pleasure there; nothing about her that says she's enjoying being with the man beside her.

Once, I wouldn't have noticed that either.

Garcias holds out a polite hand, gesturing her to the restaurant, but the gesture has the air of rote; of something one does. There is no smile to his eyes. No affection for his partner. The woman is window-dressing.

As the four enter the restaurant, the *maître de* steps smartly forward, gesturing the couple through, his manner obsequious, ignoring the heavies. "We have of course reserved your table, Mr Garcias."

He snaps his fingers and a waiter comes dashing over with a bottle, ice-bucket and stand. "I had your usual Bollinger ready for you, but of course if you prefer something else..."

Garcias grunts a 'No,' and the headwaiter bows and scrapes them to the table. The bodyguards stand back, looming over the other table guests, who pointedly look away.

I fork up some more of the excellent prawns.

Just the right amount of ginger and chilli...
And I wait.

*****

The scattered remains of a meal over the table, Garcias pushes his plate away, saying something to the woman, then rising...

At *last...*

... and I move quickly, also standing.

Tossing my napkin onto the tabletop, I smile at Airhead. "Excuse me, my dear." She blinks at my words, but nods as I turn for the washrooms. "I'll just be a moment."

As I stroll across, I scan the room.

Yes, Garcias is moving too.

In the bathrooms, I stand by the urinals and as Garcias enters, make as though I'm zipping up, giving him a perfunctory nod as I head for the basin, then make a show of washing my hands.

The mirror is a little unsettling: the dark hair and beard, even the eyes, of a stranger look back at me through spectacles I don't need. But also in the reflection, Garcias, his back turned to me, ducks at the knee a little then settles...

... and as he splashes onto the enamel, staring into space... Before he registers I'm behind him, I lock one arm around his neck, leaving the other hand free to retrieve the knife from the back of my belt and slide it to his groin.

My mouth close by his ear, "For the avoidance of doubt, I'll let you finish because I don't want to have to send my clothes to be laundered, but if you move *at all,* the knife right under your dick will have you sitting down to piss next time."

Garcias, still holding future generations in his hands, jerks then winces. "Who the *fuck* are you? I'll fucking have y..."

He gurgles as I tighten my arm, cutting off his air against the crease of my elbow. Then as I ease the pressure again, splutters for a moment.

"*Shush.* Be nice. This isn't a good time for you to get noisy. It might make me nervous and then my hand might slip. You wouldn't want that would you?" I nudge the blade upwards a trifle, nicking the skin.

"Want do you want? Has Vargas sent you? Is he the one that's doing it? Trying for a take-over? Are you his assassin?"

"No, I'm nothing to do with Vargas. Although I'll be paying him a visit too. And if I'd come as an assassin, you'd already be dead."

"What then? If it's kidnap and a ransom, you have no chance. I have men out there..."

"Yes, I know about your men. Now, *move*. Turn, slowly and walk over to the basin."

I shove him around, then forward and Garcias, hands clutching his groin, moves, very *carefully* to the washstand. I'm behind him, but he's measuring my reflection with murder in his eyes.

"No, you don't know me. You can let go of your dick now. But I still have the knife where it counts. Raise your right hand, *slowly*..."

With stubborn reluctance he raises the hand.

"Stretch it out more, towards the basin. Now close the fingers."

I give the knife another nudge, just enough to keep his attention where I want it. Releasing my grip on his neck, I loop a pre-prepared zip-tie around his wrist, then around the faucet.

"Grip the faucet."

He hisses, but I draw the loop tight.

"Now the other hand."

He doesn't move, so I do, again nicking delicate skin.

"*Fuck!* You bastard!"

"I see you're not circumcised. Want to try for a late operation?"

Garcias hisses through his teeth. "I'm going to fucking..."

"Just do as you're told. Hold the faucet. Both hands. Or you'll be carrying your balls out in your hat."

This time he obeys, and I lash both hands to the faucet, then add extra ties to be sure. The fingertips are turning red, but he'll not be there too long.

"What's this about? What do you want? Take the wallet if that's what you're after..."

"Shut the fuck up and *listen*. One warning, and you *only* get one. Do I have your attention?"

I have my knife right under his attention. He's breathing heavily but doesn't speak.

"You're going to close down your operations here..."

Garcias tries to whip around, but hand secured to the faucet, can't. "Are you fucking joking? You're not doing this to *me*. I have *millions* invested here. Why would I...?"

"Do I seem to you to be a man who is joking?"

His hands secured, I take the knife from his groin but set it to his neck instead. "You are *going* to close down your operations. You will release the women you already have, the boys too, and cancel the shipments for the ones planned or already en route. You have one week."

"I'm going to slit your fucking throat."

With the tip of the knife, I tilt up his chin, making him look at himself in the mirror, then slowly, I draw the edge over his Adam's apple, scoring the skin. A trickle of red mixes with beaded sweat. "I don't think you're in a position to negotiate. Do you?"

His face is mottled red and white, teeth gritted, eyes bulging.

I give him my best and brightest smile, then reaching down, deliberately fumble at his belt, unbuckling him and tugging at chinos and underwear, dragging them down.

His colour morphs to pasty. "No!"

"Calm down *Mr* Garcias. I'm *not* interested in that, but I'm leaving now." He's trembling. Whether it's fear or fury or shame, or all three, I'm not sure.

"If you're careful," I continue, "and take your time, you should able to break free of the zip ties. It'll take you a few minutes, but you'll be able to do it. *If* you shout for help, then the hotel staff are going to come in find you with your pants around your ankles looking as though you've been playing tie-me-up with the fairies. If I were you, I'd stay quiet. You've had your warning. I'm going now."

"I'm gonna fucking *gut* you."

"One week. One warning."

"Get these fucking things off me!"

Despite my warning to be quiet, Garcias' screams of fury carry through the door as I stroll back to the restaurant.

The noise obviously carries right through. As I amble my way through the dining room, the bodyguards suddenly stampede towards the bathrooms.

Then a sharp right and out through the service doors. Thirty seconds later I'm grinning as I lose myself in the crowds.

*****

James - Twenty Weeks

Stretched out on a lounger: I enjoy hot sunshine, the whisper of a quiet sea, a good book and on a tray by me, a jug and glasses, chilly enough to drip dew.
Perfect.
Close by, Richard doing much the same. Change my book for his newspaper and there's not much to choose between us.
He scans the financial news. A quick look sidelong at his headlines...
Markets rise...
Boom in housebuilding...
Richard *Hmmms* in satisfaction, then refolds the paper to read the international section.
Drugs trafficking, Afghanistan...
Organised crime, Thailand...
Gang violence, Columbia...
Can't they ever tell a good news story?
Charlotte's taken up her accustomed post by the edge of the pool, dabbling her toes, watching Michael and Beth...
Is she going to join them?
But she seems quite happy simply to watch.
She's so beautiful.
My Jade...
And my daughter... so far, only a smooth curve to her mother's belly. Beth's pregnancy is even less visible.
Beside me, Richard stirs, his voice low. "Don't they look great."
I follow his eye over the top of the newspaper...
... He is also watching the women.
"Oh, yes."
"Looking forward to it? Being a father again?"
"You have no *idea*."

Richard cocks a head to where Michael is cavorting with Beth in the water. He lowers his tone even more. "How's he doing now?"

I snort. "I think you can see that."

Richard chuckles, but then, "I'll rephrase that. How is Michael doing when he's not on a high; playing honeymoon games with Elizabeth?"

I rock my hand. "Highs and lows. I catch him sometimes, when he thinks I'm not looking, with shadows in his eyes. It's always going to be inside him, I think; the void Ben left behind. Not just the loss of his brother, but the manner of it, the betrayal."

Michael's gaze is straying from Beth towards me, his smile fading.

Time to change the subject...

I reach for the jug to refill my glass, but my phone *bings* an interruption, vibing the tabletop.

Who'd be messaging me now?

They all know I'm on vacation

Richard's paper lowers further, and he frowns across the top. "Someone bothering you when they shouldn't?"

But I'm already checking the screen. "No. It's an alert from my banking app."

A purchase has been made at Dorothea's babywear...

I hold up the mobile, displaying the screen. "Mitch is enjoying herself I'd say."

He lifts sunglasses, squinting against the sun as he peers across, then chuckles. "Peanut's not going to be short of clothes is she."

"Not with Mitch in charge of the shopping, no."

He eyes my glass. "What is that you're drinking?"

"Tinto de verano" Then, to his blank expression, "Red wine spritzer in your terms. Traditional summer drink where I grew up. Want some?"

"Sounds good."

The liquid fizzes pink as I pour for Richard, then top up my own.

He sips, then sips again. "Good stuff. Just dry enough. Just sweet enough. Shame the girls can't have any." Another sip. "Any more of this?"

"There's plenty of red wine and mixers in the house."

I lie back again, return to my reading, book in one hand, tumbler in the other... How is Jack Reacher going to get himself out of trouble this time?

Stretched out like this, baked by the heat, even the ache in my leg has subsided into the background. As the heat brings blood to my skin, I wipe iced condensation over my neck and face.

Aaahhhh...

My phone *bings* another announcement. Book in hand, I reach for the mobile with the other, thumbing the screen to life...

... Then cough out a mouthful of wine

What the fuck's she buying at that price?

Richard refills my glass, a smile creasing his eyes. "Your bank account creaking?"

"Do you know a store called 'And So To Bed'?"

"Nursery furniture. Cots, changing tables, storage hampers. That kind of thing. *Veeerrry* expensive on the scale of things. Elizabeth's been looking around there. Mitch having fun?"

"I'd say so, yes."

"*Expensive* fun?"

Hmmm...

He's hiding a smile behind his glass. "Did you put a limit on the card you gave her?"

"No. I told her to spend whatever she wanted."

"Does she know you get phone alerts?"

"I didn't mention it."

"You going to stop her?"

"Wouldn't dream of it. There's nothing I'd rather be spending money on, even if it's Mitch doing the spending."

The phone *bings* again and Richard explodes into laughter. "What is it this time?"

Perplexed, I stare at the alert. "Richie's artist supplies."

"Art supplies? What's that about?"

"You tell me."

She is being a busy girl...

"That card may have been a tactical error, James. I think you're in for an expensive afternoon. I think Mitch may be taking you literally."

"Suits me. I want her to. When I was married to Marlene, I spent all my time working to keep up with her spending. I barely got to see Georgie when she was small. I intend to enjoy Peanut's younger years. And, if her mother can prise Charlotte into a maternity-wear store as she expands, I'm all for it."

*****

James - Twenty-One Weeks

The last summer holiday we spent at the beach house ended very differently: Charlotte leaving for university, Michael and I almost bereft despite knowing she would return to us.

But *this* time...

There's something great about returning Home after even the best of vacations. In the days after my divorce, I didn't have a home. I just lodged in one dismal apartment after another, following the work and keeping my costs down. Even when I was married to Marlene, I never thought of the place I lived as *Home*. It was simply the place where Marlene deposited all the crap she spent so much money on.

But now, it's different.

When Michael first mooted buying the old hotel and the mess of tumbledown buildings that went with it, his priority was to provide a home for Charlotte. But over the time we have been here, it has become *Home*; for all of us, and to an extent I never imagined.

As we curve into the drive, Charlotte cranes through the window. "Wonder how the veggie patches are coming on? Hope the weeds haven't taken over. It's hard now, bending down, if I have to clear them."

Michael speaks from the back seat. "I'll send some help across from the hotel. They're using the produce in the kitchens. It won't hurt them to put in a few hours."

"Is that alright? They..."

"That's what they're paid for, Charlotte."

They're still talking: inconsequential chatter. The words don't really mean anything. It's the *connection* that's important.

My beautiful pregnant wife. My friend. Our home.

Does it get any better?

We crunch up to the front and Michael taps me on the shoulder. "I'll bring in the luggage. You get Charlotte settled and the kettle on."

"Sounds good to me."

As I help Charlotte up and out from her seat, Mitch bursts out from the front door. Charlotte breaks away from me, the two running to meet each other: Well, Mitch runs. Charlotte doesn't quite waddle...

Yet...

... but it's not exactly graceful...

Flinging their arms around each other...

"You're looking *wonderful*, Jenny..."

"We had a *great* time..."

More chatter. Again, the words aren't what's important. Over the back of the car, hefting out suitcases, Michael exchanges grins with me.

Mitch smooths a hand over Charlotte's face, standing back to look her up and down. The hand strokes over her stomach. "The holiday's done you good."

"It has. But it's *so* good to be back."

Mitch takes her by the hand, leading her indoors. "Come on inside. I wasn't sure if you would have eaten. I've made sandwiches and salad."

Michael strides in behind us, dumping luggage in the hall. "Hi Mitch. You should have come with us. You have enjoyed it."

"I've enjoyed myself anyway." Her eyes flick to me, uncertainly, then away again. "I'll make your coffee, shall I, and you can tell me about it."

In the kitchen, the coffee-maker pops and splutters. Mitch stands close by, crossing, uncrossing and re-crossing her arms, occasionally looking at me then her gaze sliding away again.

"And what have you been doing with yourself Mitch?"

She clears her throat. "Er, I um... I made rather *free* with your card."

Michael looks up from a triangle of ham sandwich, crusts removed, then turns away, hiding a smile.

"I *know* that, Mitch."

"Um... perhaps I got a bit carried away... But there were so many lovely things and... And it *was* for Jenny... And..."

"Mitch, I am *not* angry. I gave you the card intending you to use it. But I will admit, I'm curious to see what you've been doing with it."

Her face lights up. "I'll show you. It's upstairs."

Offering her my arm, I help Charlotte up from her seat. She snatches up a sandwich in mid-motion, eating it on the move. Michael polishes off his in two bites, grabs three more and follows.

Mitch opens the door to the nursery, standing back to let us in. "I hope you don't mind. I know I should have asked first, but..."

As Charlotte steps inside, she stands, raising hands to her cheeks. "Oh. My. *God.*"

And I step into a room out of some fairy-tale.

It's not quite finished. In one corner, a stepladder, hung with buckets and brushes, stands on sheeting draped over the carpet. On the wall close by, a unicorn runs; the flanks a simple outline, but with the detail of head, watching eye and rippling mane complete.

It's part of a rainbow herd, galloping, multi-coloured across one wall, flamboyant with colour. Who knew that unicorns are bird-blue, primrose yellow and apple-green? With horns in gold, silver and pearl?

One tosses its head to the winged horse above them. My mouth hanging open, I can almost hear the neigh of greeting to its flying sibling.

By the smaller side-window, a water sprite sits by a pool, apparently deep in conversation with the mermaid beside her, green-gold tail tucked neatly under. From a lily-pad close by a frog nods in apparent agreement.

Nods?

I move, shifting my perspective from one side to another.

Yes, the damn thing's *nodding.*

How the hell's she done that?

Looking closely, there's a small raised area on the plasterwork, the frog painted over the top, giving just enough dimension to the head that, as I move, it moves with me.

It is astonishingly well done.

Michael, knuckles on hips, turns in circles, whistling in air. "I thought what you did in the creche was good, Mitch, but this is *outstanding*."

Mitch shifts from one foot to the other and back again. "You like it? Jenny?"

Her hands still pressed to her face, "Oh, God, Mom. I love it. I absolutely *love* it. Thank you."

And a smile finally breaks over Mitch's face. "I did get a bit carried away. I only intended to do a few stencils…"

She waves to a corner of the room where green foliage and vast red flowers, hibiscus perhaps, scramble upward and across the ceiling. Hummingbirds hover by the blooms, dipping in. "…But they were a bit dull, so I painted them properly. Then I thought a little girl might like more…"

A mobile hangs from the ceiling, dangling butterflies and little birds in brilliant colours; stars, crescent moons and lace-winged fairies. I touch one of the fairies, trying for a better look and the whole thing spins slowly, a mass of tiny bells catching the light and tinkling.

"You like it?" Mitch is blinking again, biting her lip.

"It's lovely. I've never seen anything quite like it. Where did you buy it?"

"I didn't buy it. I made that one. There were lots on sale, but I couldn't find one I liked so…"

A rocking chair sits in a corner by the window; painted pale cream, but with leaves in soft-green vining up the legs and back., draped in soft fabrics. Charlotte strokes the timber.

Mitch moves to stand by her. "I thought it would be nice when you're feeding Peanut, to be able to look out."

"Mom, it's just perfect."

It's the only word. Perfect.

A fairy-tale nursery for a little girl.

My little girl.

"Thank you, Mitch. It's beautiful." A hand on one shoulder, I kiss her cheek. "Thank you so much."

She lets out air. "I thought you might be mad at me. I know I let loose with that card you gave me. I was worrying that..."

I place a finger in her lips. "There is *nothing* I would rather spend money on. Thank you for doing it on my behalf."

A slow smile blooms over her face. "I did enjoy myself. It's been such fun. Being able to buy all the things I could never afford for Jenny. I always had to make do for her. Or do without."

"So much the better."

"I made you a shopping list of what I bought."

"Mitch, I don't need it..."

But she presses it into my hand.

Crib...

Changing Table. ...

Storage Baskets. ...

Dresser. ...

Mobile. ...

Rocking Chair. ...

Clothes Hamper.

Charlotte starts to sit, to try out the rocking chair, then straightens up again, hands pressing to the small of her back. "Back in a minute."

"You alright?"

"I need to pee."

Later, I return, strolling around the fairy wonderland Mitch has created for her grand-daughter.

Life is good.

Life is *perfect*.

What could go wrong?

The birth... The delivery...

Modern hospitals.

Modern medicine.

We'll be with her, me and Michael. The best doctor. The best mid-wife.

The best of everything.

She'll be fine.

*****

James - Twenty-Nine Weeks

What's she looking for?

Standing in the kitchen doorway, I watch as Charlotte, her back to me, rummages through the shelves of the store cupboard.

The latest tee-shirt is already tight, rolling up a little over her expanded waistline as she stretches upwards. Muttering to herself, she works through tins and jars then, with an audible *Mmmm...* takes a plastic container from the top shelf. Unclipping the lid, she extracts a slab of chocolate brownie.

Caught in the act.

"That will be your third this morning, Charlotte."

She jolts, looking over her shoulder at me, pressing fingers to her mouth as she chews then gulps. "Michael brought them over from the hotel for me when I said I fancied something sweet."

Stepping across to her, I take the cake from her hand and replace it in the box, minus one bite. "He brought enough for *everyone*. I don't think he intended you to eat the lot yourself."

She drops her eyes. "If you don't want me to eat them," she mutters, "then put them somewhere I can't get them."

"Fine." I clip the lid back on the box and place it on the ground at her feet.

She leans forward, trying to see over her own stomach. "That's not fair," But there's laughter in her voice.

"Life's not fair. I'm not having Peanut coming out chocolate-coated." I reach for the bowl on the table, then holding her by the wrist, slap an apple in her palm. "If you want something sweet, eat fruit."

She takes a bite from the apple, then waddling to the table, sits, legs splayed, to take another. "We can't keep calling her Peanut. She's got to have a proper name sometime."

"Got anything in mind?"

"Actually, yes. I thought... well, she's my daughter and your daughter, but Michael helped and he's going to be *officially* the father so..."

"You don't have to give me the sales pitch. What's in your mind?"

"I thought, Michael's mom; she's called Cara."

Cara?

Cara...

"Cara." I roll the word around my mouth.

"What do you think?"

"Cara... Yes, I like that. It's a Spanish word, did you know?"

"What does it mean?"

"Expensive."

She laughs. "Well, that certainly true with everything we're spending. But I looked up the name too. It also means 'loved'."

"Loved? Cara it is then."

She smiles, wide and bright. "Do we tell him yet?"

I give her a squeeze around the shoulders. "Let's keep it as a surprise, eh."

*****

Charlotte - Thirty Weeks

The stretchy black leggings bulge at my waist. Tugging at the front of my Hippopotamus tee-shirt, I try to draw it down to cover my stomach. With a stretch, it *just* goes over and I survey the result in the mirror.

When were my tits ever this size?

I'm blessed with large breasts, just good luck on my part I suppose; an inheritance from my mother. But now they are *huge*.

And my belly protrudes beyond them.

Well beyond them.

I suck in, trying to draw in my stomach. Of course, it won't go and as I release my breath, the tee-shirt abruptly rolls itself back up my stomach to sit like a belt under my swinging boobs...

Well, that's one way of supporting them...

Defeated, I take Elephant tee-shirt from my wardrobe and try it for size. It looks odd, the label dangling at the back, but the fit is depressingly good.

I'm lying to myself. It's tight.

It still stretches over my belly. Tugging at it, trying to settle it to drape a little more loosely, but the horrible thing creases into lines over my widest middle.

And there's *weeks* to go yet.

*How **big** am I going to get?*

Click!

I whirl, in time to see my Master, still laughing as he holds up his phone, displaying the screen and the photo he just took.

"Oh, God no. Wipe it, please."

"*Why* for heaven's sake?" He examines the screen. "It's a lovely photo. Just caught the moment." He scissors fingers, zooming in and his smile *glows*.

Then as he looks back to me, "Charlotte, *really*. I just wanted to catch you stroking yourself over the stomach like that as you saw yourself in the mirror." The smile returns, dancing around his eyes. "You look *amazing*." He lays a hand on my belly, stroking the bump. "*Both* of you."

"But I'm... I'm... so *fat*... and I feel ugly... And my boobs are too big. And none of my real clothes fit any more... And... I'm so clumsy. I waddle when I walk and... I thought maybe... maybe..." And..."

I must sound ridiculous...

And I shut up.

He exhales, looking away from me, then pulls me into his arms.

He murmurs, "You are *not* fat and ugly. You are pregnant and *beautiful*. Pregnant with our beautiful daughter. And she is going to grow up to be as brave and intelligent and *beautiful* as her mother. And *I* cannot *wait* for her to be born so I can see that happening. But for now, I am very happy to watch my *beautiful, pregnant* wife getting ready for all that."

"You're sure?" My voice trembles as I cast across to the mirror where, somehow, my Master's arms don't wrap around me as widely as they used to.

"Oh, Charlotte. My Jade-Eyes. You really are being..." He rubs the back of his head. "*Why* are you so insecure about this? You have two men who love you more than life itself and a third who's only reason for not feeling the same is that his wife is your cousin."

He halts. Then his tone changes.

The Dom...

"Get down."

"What?"

"You heard me." He snaps the instruction. "Bend over the end of the bed. Support yourself on your arms. No pressure on your stomach."

"Master..."

But he turns me, positions me, pushes me down at the shoulders. "Your weight on your hands. That's it."

From behind me the snap of leather and the rasp off metal. "If I have to do something as absurd as prove to you that I still want you just as much as I ever did, then it's easy enough."

He slips thumbs into the waistband of the leggings, pulling it clear of my belly then tugging down.

"Panties too. *Step*."

He yanks the lot free of me as I raise one foot then the other. "Now..." The heat of his groin presses to my hips, the warmth of his chest to my spine, as he strokes down my arms. "... You're comfortable? Supported properly?"

"Yes, Master."

"Good. Now... Relax, and remind yourself that you are *loved*..." And with that, his body heat leaves my skin...

... replaced by the glide of his fingers at the back of my knees. *Aaahhh...*

My legs buckle, but his arm snaps around me, supporting me. "Careful..." And as I steady myself. "Want to try that again?"

"Yes, Master. Please. It just caught me by surprise."

He curves around me, pressing a kiss into my neck. "Good girl."

I think he squats down behind me, warm breath washing over my rear, but I don't think it's deliberate...

... *Yet*...

... simply a measure of his position behind me.

And this time, at the sweet/tormenting touch of fingernails over skin, drawing between upper calves and lower thighs, I hold myself, huffing air as electricity skitters up and between my thighs, centering into my sex and setting my clit pulsing.

"Much better... Wet already. That's my girl..."

I want him to move into more sexual territory, up and in, and I shuffle, spreading my ankles...

The fingers freeze. "Who is Master here?"

My flash quivering, "You are."

"So, *wait*."

The fingers resume, a small journey, digging in oh-so-slightly to sensitive skin and jangling nerves...

My huffing turns to gasping and now the heat comes from inside, blooming into my purring pussy...

And as the nails draw up higher, easing a path into the delicate skin of my inner thighs...

... and *up*...

... and *in*...

A hot mouth... hot lips... a hot tongue... plant themselves over me, sucking, licking, probing...

Then station themselves on my bud, winding circles, nudging the base, swiping over the tip...

It's exquisite. Agonising. Ecstatic. Unbearable...

What's the sound I'm making?

I have no idea. A yell? A howl? A scream...

I don't know, but it is born somewhere deep in my throat to emerge as a kind of guttural wail as I try to hang onto enough sanity and control to keep myself supported over the bed.

Something moves and, straining my neck a little to see:

It's Michael, smiling as he seats himself on the edge of the bed. "I swear, Babe, if I was surrounded by canon going off, I'd hear you singing out like that." He grins. "Sheer catnip."

Behind me, my Master shifts, I think standing up. "Michael. Perfect timing. Charlotte here seems to be of the opinion that being pregnant has made her... What were the words? Ah, yes. Fat and ugly."

From my semi-up-side-down position, I see Michael's eyes roll. He looks away, then back again, shaking his head. But his voice is soft. "You're an idiot, Charlotte." His gaze slants off and behind me. "I take it that's the point you're about to prove?"

"You could say that, yes." A pause. "Where's Mitch?"

Michael thumbs across to the window. "We were chatting outside. Then she suddenly made her excuses, grabbed a paintbrush and set off for the hotel."

"Good." And with no preamble, fingers from either side open me and my Master pushes in and home.

I yelp, and Michael rockets close, holding me under the arms, supporting me with his body as my Master fucks me, not hard, but thoroughly.

Ohhh.... Goddd....

My body rocks with his rhythm, and Michael's with me. From the fore, he slips fingers between my thighs, tweaking my bud. "You gonna come for us, Babe?"

My Master withdraws, my pussy contracting around the abrupt emptiness, and a hard hand swats across my ass. "I have *never* heard anything so *fucking* ridiculous, Charlotte."

A hand comes across the other side, harder now, stinging. "If it weren't for your condition, I would punish you to straighten out your thinking. As it is, I will assume that you are doing too much of that thinking with your hormones instead of your head."

Another slap, again harder and on the same spot, and I gasp. "And once we are past this..." *Another* slap... "... and I can act freely with your *beautiful* body... I am going to fuck you 'til you need a baby-sitter for a *week,* while you learn to walk again after I've done with you."

And he plunges in again, filling me.

Michael is playing havoc with my clit, arousal sparking and stabbing and jabbing through to my core, tightening me around my Master's cock as he pounds me. My face heated, I'm dripping sweat over Michael...

"Come on, Babe..."

I'm liquifying, melting...

And with a yell, I *Come.*

A hand tugs at my hair, lifting my face and Michael fastens his mouth over mine, still playing a virtuoso performance on my bud while from behind, my Master fucks me hard.

And as I shudder to a dripping, gasping halt, he groans, his hips grinding against me.

Still panting, he withdraws, releasing me and I roll onto the bed, both my husbands watching me.

My Master's voice is dry. "Is that enough proof for you?" Then his eyes widen, and he points. "Look!"

"What? What is it?"

I swing around then realise where both he and Michael are looking, and my gaze drops to join theirs.

And there, where Elephant tee-shirt stretches over me, drawn tight, quite clearly visible is the outline of a tiny handprint, pressing outwards.

My Master, grinning delightedly, snatches up his phone again, opening the camera and flicking on to video. The tiny hand moves. "She's waving! Peanut is waving 'Hello.'"

Michael simply stares, mesmerised. Then he reaches to touch. His outstretched forefinger is large than the tiny handprint, but he rubs gently at it. "Hello, Peanut."

I flop back. "Gotta say, Guys. She feels more like Coconut these days"

*****

James - Thirty-Two Weeks

I perch a hip on an old stone wall, looking down the mountain, the meadows, the lake. The weather is fine and warm; late Summer drawing into Autumn and...

Life is *good*.

I have the woman I love, friendship, money, rewarding work, a wonderful home and, in only a few months, a new baby daughter.

I raise my glass in a silent toast.

Looking forward to meeting you Cara...

My cup overflows.

Where's Charlotte?

I'd like her with me, just to share this moment.

Heaving myself upright, I go in search of her. I move easily. With the sunshine, even my bad leg is behaving itself.

I find her in the restaurant, by the big picture window that looks down the mountain to the lake, Charlotte sits between Michael's Gran, his Aunty Edna and another of the tribe that I don't recognise...

Or do I?

I have trouble separating out the legion of old harpies occupying the upper echelons of Michael's family, but I do vaguely recall Michael threatening me with a nasty outbreak of his family sometime this week. My mind must have drawn a discreet veil over the memory.

But now, from the far side of the restaurant, I pause...

Charlotte should be enjoying herself; the centre of attention, everyone making a fuss of her.: the new Mom-To-Be. But she doesn't look happy.

What's wrong?

As I draw closer...

One of the three engulfs a sandwich whole, champing with badly fitting false teeth. Another is in full flow. "... and I was in labour for thirty-four hours with our Neville you know. *Thirty-four* hours, would you believe it. And every minute of it was absolute hell. They didn't have things like epee-doo-rals then, of course and...

She is cut short by the third. ... Oh, those epidurals aren't all they're cut out to be. Our Agnes had one of those. They stuck the needle straight into her spine and it didn't do a *thing* to help. Didn't take the pain away at all. Just meant she couldn't push for three hours till it wore off. And she was screaming all the way through it. And *then* she needed stitches where she split right open..." The old bag makes a gesture like she's unzipping her crotch... "Thirty-seven stitches she needed right up her... Like this..." And she zips herself back up again.

Charlotte looks stricken, blinking and swallowing. My face heats...
Jade...
A bit of needless terror is all part of the magic of pregnancy?
*That's enough of **that**...*
The first seems set to argue, swallowing her sandwich, then...
Oh, my God...
... taking out her false teeth and setting them on the pristine white tablecloth, leans forward conspiratorially, starting to speak. "Yes, but did you hear about what happened with Nancy..."

Charlotte twists her hands together, knuckles whitening.
Schadenfreude...
I don't give a flying fuck about Nancy. "Excuse me ladies. I believe Michael is looking for Charlotte. I hope you'll excuse her."

Relief washes over her face as I take her by both hands, helping her upright. The trio of sour-faced harridans look outraged. "Can I get the waitress to bring you anything else? More coffee or tea? Another plate of sandwiches?"

"Some more of that lemon drizzle cake would be nice."

"And some extra chocolate cake," says another. "The kind with the sprinkles on."

"I'll see to it right away. Charlotte?" I offer her my arm, steering her to the exit. Then, "Just give me a moment will you."

She waits, sucking in her lips as I make for our chef, sitting in a quiet corner, sketching out menus and meal plans. "Sally, see that set of old Gorgons are kept fed and watered, would you."

She casts a measuring eye across the room to Stheno, Euryale and Medusa. "Upsetting Charlotte, are they?"

"Scaring her silly, I'd say. And enjoying doing it. Just feed them unconscious, then I can pack them in a taxi and send them home."

She drops me a wink and half a smile. "Will do."

Retrieving my quaking mermaid, I guide her out. "Don't let them upset you, Charlotte. I've checked and double-checked with the doctors. Your pregnancy is going very well, and everything is as it should be."

She ducks her head. "I'm a bit scared, Master."

Old bitches...

How much damage have they done?

I turn, and finger under her chin, tilt her face to mine. "Don't be. *Everything* is fine." I press my lips to hers. "In just a few weeks you are going to present me with our daughter. And she will grow up to be healthy, beautiful, intelligent and as brave as her mother. And *unlike* her mother, right from the beginning, she will have the best of everything that life has to offer, including a close and loving family."

She eases a little, a pale smile ghosting her lips. "I know. It's just... when I hear some of the stories..."

"Yes, it's hard for a woman giving birth. I know that. But I also know that when Cara is placed in your arms, whatever has happened, you will forget all of it. *All* you will remember is that you have the child which you wanted and which you have gifted for me."

Her smile widens. "I'm being silly, aren't I."

"No, you're not. Childbearing isn't a trivial matter. But this isn't a hundred years ago and we're not living in the third world. Everything is going to be fine." I brush her lips with mine again. "I promise you."

*****

"Mitch, can I leave Charlotte with you for a while? She's a bit upset and I need a word with Michael."

Her lips move to ask the question, but I wriggle fingers, head-pointing her to Charlotte, and without a pause, she switches lanes. "Of course you can, James. Here, Jenny, have some peppermint tea. It's wonderful for calming you down."

Now...
How to deal with this?
Tell it like it is...

Arming myself with a couple of cans of beer, I find Michael where I expect to, out by the old stables, working on, as luck would have it, the new stables.

I flip the tab on one, offer the other. "How's it going?"

"Pretty well. You could have a look around and see if it looks okay to you. You're the horse expert, not me."

I stroll around. The stables themselves are looking good with well-boarded stalls, nails and screw-heads knocked well in, decent drainage and racks for hay and feed. The tack room is spacious and airy but despite a couple of plastic crates stacked in a corner, some of the necessaries are still missing.

"We'll need racking for tack and tools, and we'll have to do something about the fencing."

He holds the can to his face, swiping condensation over cheek and neck. "Next on my list. Well, almost. The actual next is bookshelves."

More bookshelves?

I run a mental inventory of Charlotte's study. "Surely she's not run out of space already? You only installed the last lot a couple of months ago."

"Not Charlotte. Mitch." He pulls a face. "I don't know if there's a gene for bibliophilia, but if there is then you're hiring a damn carpenter when Peanut learns to read."

"Mitch? She's got you on bookshelves?"

"Take a look." He waves across to the crates. "She's already filled the space she's got and she's storing them in here."

Swigging at the beer, I prise off a lid, looking at a couple of titles.

Turn Right at Machu Picchu, Mark Adams... Lands of Lost Borders: A Journey on the Silk Road, Kate Harris... The Innocents Abroad, Mark Twain...

*A whole **stack** of Bill Bryson titles...*
Bit of a theme going on there.
Wonder if she wants to travel?
Get back to the point...

"Michael, I mean no offence, but I have to say this. I know they are your family, but you need to keep those dried-up harpies you call aunts either under control or away from Charlotte."

He jolts to attention. "Why, what's up?"

"What's *up*, is that they're scaring the bejeezus out of Charlotte. Telling her all kinds of lurid tales about childbirth."

He groans, scratching at his head. "Oh, Christ. They've not being going through those 'thousand pits of hell' delivery stories, have they?"

"Yes, they have. What with sore breasts and swollen ankles, I think she has enough to handle without Timeless Tales of Terror being inflicted on her. I'm not having her upset like that."

He leans, his weight on one arm, palm resting against the wall; looks down, looks up again. "Right!" He mutters something else under his breath.

"What was that?"

"I *said*, Interfering old bats."

"You took the words from my mouth."

He knocks back the last of his beer. "It's not even true. That side of the family pops 'em like peas from fucking pods. That's why there's so damn many of them. Leave it with me. I'll deal with it."

"How? You think they'll pay any attention to you?"

"To me? No. I'm a mere male. But they'll listen to my mother."

Suddenly feeling the ice thin below me, "How is she now?"

He looks down, apparently finding the scuffed toes of his work boots of interest. "After Ben? Not good. But she's been gradually improving with having a grandchild on the way. Something else to think about, y'know. So... she'll not be happy when son-number-two comes making complaint for the mother-to-be."

"Does she... *know* the score?"

"I've not spelled it out, no. But from her point of view, Charlotte's baby will be her grandchild. And the next one actually will be. I don't see any point at all in upsetting the applecart."

Is this the time to tell him?

Yes...

Put a smile on his face...

"Did Charlotte tell you we've decided on a name?"

He perks up. "No, she didn't. What is it?"

"You can tell your mother there's going to be another Cara Summerford in the family."

His smile breaks like a rising sun. "You're naming Peanut after my mother?"

"Seemed the least we could do. We did consider naming her after *you,* but calling her Michelle could have caused confusion..."

The pleasure on his face is a warm balm. "You think she'll be pleased?"

He wipes a palm over his face. "James, I don't think there's *anything* would please her more. Thank you, *both* of you."

"This is about the *three* of us. "

"So, next time, I'm the sperm donor and we name the baby after *your* mother?"

I rock on my toes. "You might find my mother's name a bit of a mouthful."

His head tilts back. "Go on."

"Pastora Sofia Conchetta Martina Linares"

"Yeessss... That's a mouthful. What was your father called?"

"Harry."

"We'd better hope the next one's a boy then."

*****

Klempner - Thailand

I set out early, catching the sunrise and making the most of what passes for the cool of the dawn here. Even given the purpose of my trek, I can take the time to look around and appreciate the beauty of my surroundings.

I've travelled pretty much everywhere that is reachable without being Shackleton or Hillary, and while it is something I enjoy, the actual 'travel' part of travelling is usually uninteresting. There's only so much variety in cabins and airports.

But this is different.

There is something about walking: hiking to your destination, connecting with the landscape, that makes the journey more real. And it doesn't get any realer than it is here.

So early in the day, hiking up the trail through verdant forest, high up the mountain; sun-slanted mist weaves through the canopy.

Trail over-plays the track I'm following. No human laid this route. Some animal probably made it, but of course, most of them are much closer to the ground than I am. From my six foot vantage point I hack my way through dense vegetation. The machete is seeing sterling service, but my wrist is aching already.

What kind of animal?
Wild pigs maybe?
Not an appealing thought...

I don't much fancy meeting a wild pig except with an apple stuck in its mouth. I've seen versions of them all over the world and none of them were sweet little pink things saying *Oink*. They're dangerous creatures; wickedly tusked and fast moving. Omnivorous too. If they get you down, there won't be a corpse to be found by the time they're finished.

But hopefully the local version will be sleeping in daylight. In any case, most wildlife doesn't come looking for trouble. Or if it does, a machete isn't a bad defence against unwanted attentions.

Birds and, I think some kind of monkey, screech and howl above me. I can't see much of the local wildlife other than, way up, the odd flapping wing between one tree and the next. But the noise is cacophonous.

Just now, the temperature in the low seventies, the walking isn't bad. But the humidity is climbing and sweat gathers between my shoulder blades, streaking my shirt and making it harder to stay cool.

And the temperature is rising.

Here under the canopy it shouldn't get too hot, at least as the glass measures it, but the moisture in the air is draining. My lips taste salty and my eyes sting.

I can't do anything about the rucksack, other than packing it properly in the first place for balance and to be sure I don't have cutlery jamming into my spine, but the rifle is a different matter. I pause a few seconds to shift it from one shoulder to the other, rubbing at the ache.

Getting too old for this game?

I slap at an arm.

Fucking things...

What do these things eat when they can't get hobbit?

The choice is to leave my arms bare and get bitten. Or cover up and swelter. I settle for the bites but slather on citronella gel...

Maybe it'll poison the little bastards...

Then I stop to pluck thorns that have somehow penetrated my pants and boots: in theory, the toughest trail clothing available. But the local vegetation is unimpressed by the claim, merely rising to the challenge of spiking the unwary.

The sun rises higher, gleaming green and gold through a shimmering roof of leaves. I could wish to be in better mood to appreciate it, but sweat trickles down my face, itching abominably.

*How does anyone **stand** having a fucking beard all the time?*
I'm beginning to dream of a razor and foam.
I'm well up the mountain now.
Shouldn't it get cooler with altitude?
But with the heavy exercise, my load and the ever-climbing humidity, the blood rises up my neck and face and somehow, the bloody boots have doubled their weight.
How far have I come?
I take out a phone, opening the mapping app, scissoring and zooming.
Not so far as I'd have liked...
The heat is intense now. Sweat streams uselessly down my forehead, not cooling, only soaking my clothes as it trickles down. My eyes are watering and as I swipe over my face, my palm tastes briny.
The sun continues to climb, hovering in its blue dome, assaulting tree and insect and me. The earlier howl and squawk has stilled. Even the insects are quieter. I stand, hands on hips, simply breathing, reaching for air that, against all sense, isn't there.
What's that?
I freeze, cocking my head, *listening*.
The sound of running water...
No, the *roar* of running water.
Stepping smartly, out, breaking from the trail, I follow the sound, until with shocking suddenness, the trees open in front of me.
The luxuriant foliage clears. To one side, the forest stretches as far as the eye can see. To the other, a waterfall.
And I stand, looking up, gaping.
'Waterfall' doesn't do it justice. *Waterfalls* would be more correct: dozens, scores, even hundreds of them; all interconnected and weaving from one to another. Level by level, from hundreds of feet above, stretching wide all around me, tier upon tier of water cascades in

cataracts and streaming ribbons, dancing and frothing as it falls to the river before continuing its journey to the sea far below.

Water as clear as crystal, clean as a maiden's conscience, rushes in a never-ending dream.

All other sound is obliterated by the song of the falls. My heart thumps under my ribs, but I hear nothing but the water.

How can this not be in the tourist brochures?

Did I simply miss it in overly hasty research on the area?

On the other hand, given the strenuous approach, few but the most determined would reach here.

And I stand, simply gazing at a vision of heaven.

Fine spray fills the air: not the cloying humidity of only a few minutes before, but a refreshing mist that casts rainbows arcing above me and washes, clean and invigorating, over my face and hands and arms.

Sucking at my cheeks, I check the phone again for my position.

Then I glance up at the enemy sun.

What's the hurry?

I'll work better for a rest...

... and a wash...

Stooping, I run fingers through the water. It laves my fingers, caressing and cooling...

No competition...

Then havering, I look around.

What if I'm seen?

It is beyond belief that this place isn't known...

Surely there must be visitors?

Tourists... Gawkers...

There's always someone willing to make a ridiculous journey to see the truly unique.

And sure enough, as I look, I see another trail, much broader than my own, well-trodden. There are even tire tracks.

But that water is calling me.

I wander the edges, searching, stepping from one polished rock to another, placing my boots carefully...

No place for a twisted ankle...

Away from the main torrent of falling water, a clear pool sits to one side, deep and wide, edged by rocks polished smooth, and still, save for the small eddying swirls which sparkle and spin in the sunshine. And better, it vanishes under a rock overhang, curtained off by cascading water, well away from any possible passer-by. Perfect shelter.

Stepping with care, I edge along a craggy edge. The water has long ago polished away any crevices for fingers, and moss, thick and green coats much of it. But snatched handfuls of ferns balance me as I skip over one slick stepping-stone to another until, with shocking suddenness, I find myself out of the sunlight and in a dim green space, the pool at my feet screened by frothing water.

I heave, shrugging off both pack and rifle. The pack drops with a *clunk*. The rifle I lean against a rock wall. Not that it's fragile, but a pro looks after his equipment.

Stripping off the sweat-stained vest, I toss the stinking thing to one side. Boot laces next...

Aaahhhh...

I kick them off and fresh air kisses my feet. The rest of my clothes follow.

Naked, I stand on a flattish rock, and *leaping*, I dive, cutting into the water...

... then surface, spluttering and gasping, snatching sweet, stinging air into shuddering, heaving lungs

"Fuck!"

Christ, but that's cold!

Puffing, I stand, waist high in the water, then with a yell and a laugh, duck again, swimming long strokes across the pool and back again.

An hour later, clothed again, I sit by the pool edge, just on the edge of my water-curtain cover. Sipping from a tin mug, I watch the pageant of the waters. A trail bar in one hand, I take a bite, then chewing, watch the spectacle. Occasionally, I survey my surroundings.

No other people in sight...

Still... Thailand...

It has a reputation as a different kind of tourist destination.

Another five minutes; I check my watch, refill the water bottle from the pool, then, repacking, I heave up the backpack, slinging the rifle back over a shoulder, and set off again along my pig-trail.

Uphill all the way...

*****

James – Thirty-Five Weeks

I stride into the kitchen fanning smoke away from my face.

Charlotte stands by the grill, the pan a grisly mess of charcoal and curled-up charcoal.

She bursts into tears. "I burned the toast."

Briskly dipping a tea-towel into the sink, I drape it over the grill-pan, then pull her into a hug. "It's *not* a disaster. No harm's been done. And we *can* afford another loaf." I guide her to the table. "Now sit down and I'll make you some more toast. What would you like on it? Honey? Marmalade? Cheese?"

She sniffles, her face low. "Just butter, please." Then she jerks up again. "I'm *really* sorry. I didn't mean..."

"Charlotte... Charlotte..." I draw up a chair by her, pull her face to mine, kiss her forehead. "You have it all out of proportion. Come on, see the funny side." I cast down. "Look, Scruffy will eat your burnt offering if no-one else will."

Then I regret my words. The pint-sized mongrel grins up ingratiatingly, displaying more teeth than the average wolf and drops...

Um...

... a dried-up frog at our feet.

Charlotte bursts into laughter. "Oh, *God*. That was just what I needed."

And at that moment, the door bangs open and the kitchen is suddenly *teeming* with dogs as Kirstie's four make a mass entrance.

Can five dogs teem?

Yes.

Time to tell Kirstie to move 'em on. She's well enough now...

Still... turn every problem into an opportunity...

I stand, snatching up the cremated remains of Charlotte's intended snack and hurl the lot out of the back door. The canine contingent follows the mess *en masse*, shedding hair, slobber and mud in equal measure as they depart.

"See," I say. "Just a cheap way of feeding the dogs."

Charlotte chuckles, looking much more herself, then the smile fades and she turns pensive again.

"Charlotte, talk to me. What's upsetting you?"

She looks down, scuffing at the tiles, looking like some little girl admitting to stealing cookies. All that's missing is the pigtails.

"Charlotte?"

"Master..." She twines finger, hands resting over the bump of her stomach.

An ugly thought grips me.

Surely not?

"Charlotte, you're not regretting this are you?" I tilt her face up to mine, eye-pointing down to her stomach. "Having second thoughts?"

Her eyes widen. "Oh, no... Master... *No.*"

Thank God for that.

"No, never. I *so* wanted to do this. And I still do. It's..." And her face drops again.

I pull her into my arms, resting my chin on the top of her head. "Jade Eyes. Talk to me. Tell me what's wrong. How can I help make it right for you if I don't know what's troubling you?"

She blurts out the words. "I'm scared."

"Scared? Of the pregnancy? Of becoming a mother?"

"The labour. It's..." Her face drops into her hands. "Oh, *God*. I'm terrified of what's coming."

Those fucking old women...

They're coming nowhere near again 'til this is over...

Dropping back to perch on the table edge, I take a couple of deep breaths. "This isn't like you, Charlotte. You're the most fearless woman I know. What exactly are you so scared of?"

"I'm scared of the pain. And that Cara might not be... as she should be. I'm scared they might have to cut me open to get her out and I'll be scarred and that you won't... I'm scared I won't be a good mother. They say when you had a bad upbringing that you pass it on, don't they..."

She plunges on, spilling her terrors and I wait quietly for the tide of worry and fear to run its course.

Some of it I've heard already. Some is new to me. A part of me wants to laugh it off. Woman have been doing this for as long as there have been women.

But...

What do I know about how it feels to be pregnant?

Your body running riot... Hormones out of control...

Dependent...

Partially helpless...

And knowing that even the easiest labour is a time of pain and anxiety...

*And it's her **first**.*

"Charlotte, you trust me surely? My feelings for you? My judgement?"

Streaming tears, she lifts her face to me. "Of *course* I do."

"Then trust me now. You're going to be fine. *Cara* is going to be fine. Your body is raging with hormones, running away with your head. You're letting your imagination sweep you away. *Everything* is perfectly normal, as it should be."

She wipes her face with the heel of a hand. "Yes, I know all that. At least, my head know it. It's just..."

I take her hands, placing them together and sandwiching between my own. "Charlotte, I can't imagine what it feels like to be a woman, to have another life growing inside you. But I *can* understand that, as you are now, you're feeling dependent; helpless even. And that's not easy for you. But I'm *here*. Michael is *here*. For *you*. When it really comes down to it, this is what men are *for;* to look after pregnant women, mothers, children."

I kiss her forehead. "I will *always* be here for you. As long as I draw breath, I will be here for you."

*****

James - Thirty-Six Weeks

Only a few more weeks...
 I can barely contain myself.
 Her mother is still working hard to get Charlotte to buy *some* new clothes... Michael and I watch the conversation with the fascination of a couple of popcorn-popping movie addicts.
 Mitch, her arms folded, one toe tapping... "... After all, Christmas is coming, and you will want something nice to wear, won't you?"
 "I suppose."
 "And, you'll want James and Michael to see you at your best, don't you? For Christmas?"
 "Cara might have been born by then."
 "Even if she has, you won't go back to your original size overnight. You're not a bicycle tire."
 "I suppose."
 "So..." Mitch spins on me, a searing whirlwind of maternal authority. "So, James and Michael can come too, *can't* they."
 Michael rises from his seat as though rocket-propelled... "Gotta finish the drainage in the stable yard..." ... and is gone.
 Damn!
 Mitch's smile zeros in on me...
 "I have some work to do..."
 "But you said at breakfast you were going to have a quiet day..."
 Bank up the fire...
 My armchair...
 A good book...
 Maybe a brandy...
 Mitch dangles the car keys at me. "I'll sit in the back. Jenny needs all the space she can get right now.

Shoe-horning Charlotte into the front seat of the car, I drive us to Mitch's intended destination; a department store with a large range of designer maternity wear and eye-watering prices.

"Don't worry, James," she murmurs. "It's just the one dress, so she has something decent to wear over the holiday."

"I'm paying for this, then?"

She dimples, so beautifully. "But you must be *so* tired of seeing her in leggings and tee-shirts?"

True...

"Good. Then you can stay with her in the fitting room and tell her she looks beautiful while I go and pick out dresses for her to try."

Oh, joy...

*****

Two hours and a score of outfits later, I'm losing the will to live.

Charlotte examines herself in the mirror, side on, with disfavour. In fact, the dress looks fabulous on her. Mitch's eye for design doesn't stop at painting and the gown displays beautifully my scowling beauty, emphasising her height and her much-expanded bosom, but draping smoothly over her extravagant midriff.

She turns, scrutinizing herself from the other side, then eyes me. "Do I look fat?"

"You look pregnant."

She grimaces. "*Yes*, but do I look fat?"

"You look *pregnant*."

"I *do* look fat."

If that lip sticks out any further, I'll use it as a bookshelf...

I slide my arms around her, which isn't as easy as it once was, kissing the top of her head. "*No*. You look pregnant. And lovely as ever with it."

"But I've gone all... There's so *much* of me." Her words end on a wail.

"Well, what did you expect? Apply some basic engineering principles."

She stills in my embrace, looking up into my face. "Engineering principles? What are you talking about, Master?"

"If you want to carry extra passengers, you have to increase the payload, expand the stores and the catering facilities, and install extra seating."

And she finally bursts out laughing, slapping me on the chest. "'Course you do. I'm being silly, aren't I?"

"Very silly." And I plant a kiss on her forehead. "Charlotte, you look wonderful. Do you like the dress? If you do, you'll be wearing it for Christmas dinner."

"Yes, I do." Her eyes are merry and bright. "Master, I'm sorry..."

Then as she shifts in my arms and I realise her intent... "*Don't* kneel, for God's sake. I'd need a block and tackle to get you back on your feet, and I doubt they supply them in the ladies-wear department."

And again, she bursts out laughing.

That's my Jade-Eyes...

"Let's get you out of this and tell your mother she can call back the expeditionary forces. How about tea and cakes now?"

And her arm hooked into mine, we're still laughing and joking as we step back into the main store...

... and I all but walk into Georgie... My daughter, tall, slimly built, dark-haired and dark-eyed like me.

Her eyes widen, her hands coming up as we almost bounce into each other. "Whoa! Dad..." She frowns. "What on earth are you doing *here?*"

Then she seems to realize Charlotte is with me. "Who...?" And her eyes drop to my Jade's protruding belly.

Now what?

Tell it as it is...

"Charlotte, this is my daughter, Georgie. Georgie, this is Charlotte. My wife."

Georgie's mouth opens and closes. "Your *wife?* But..."

Charlotte offers her hand. "Pleased to meet you, Georgie. James has spoken so much about you."

Georgie doesn't take the hand, instead simply staring at Charlotte's stomach. "But... she's just a kid. And she's *pregnant*..."

"Aren't you going to congratulate me? And Charlotte?"

Georgie's face twists to anger. "What are you playing at, Dad?" Speaking as though she's not there, she jerks a thumb at Charlotte. "She's younger than I am. Don't you think you're a bit long in the tooth to be seducing children?"

Charlotte hisses, "I am *not* a child."

Can I rescue this?

"Georgie, aren't you just a little bit pleased for me? That I have a successful marriage. That I'm going to be a father again. That *you're* going to have a sister..."

"I've no idea what you thinking you're doing, Dad. This is... is..."

I lean in close to my daughter, whispering into her ear. "*Licet felix est.*" She glares at me... "And whether you like it or not, I *am* happy. Charlotte is my *wife* and Cara in there," I eye-point downwards... "... is your sister."

Georgie spits the words. "She's no sister of mine." And turning on her heel, she disappears into the milling crowds.

Charlotte's eyes are glossy. "Master, I'm so sorry. I..."

"Forget it, Charlotte. We all make our own choices. Georgie has made hers."

Mitch reappears, arms piled high. "Right, *Shoes.*"

*****

Klempner - Thailand

Hours later, my water-break is a half-forgotten dream. I'm sweaty and uncomfortable. The sun has westered beyond the treeline and shadows draw long.

It's been tough; not so far in terms of distance covered, but the going is steep and over broken ground that bizarrely, has left me with a crick in my neck from constantly looking down to watch where I place my feet.

But it's levelling out now, getting easier, and I'm leaving the treeline behind me, the trees thinning. Still hiking hard, I check the mapping app. Despite my break, I'm where I intended to be by now, the trail skirting around the mountain, more or less on a contour.

Behind me, above and to my left, the forest is thick and impenetrable. To my right, ahead of me, a sheer drop, some hundreds of feet of rocky cliff-face, has opened up the view. I look over mile upon myriad mile of forest, stretching out in waves of mountain height, valley delve and misted crevasse.

But on the edge of my vision, forward on my trek, the trail curves along its ridge towards a glimpse of the sea. Another few hundred yards and the sea, and if I have it right, my destination, will be in plain view.

Swiping at my forehead with an already-sopping rag, I gulp water, shaking the bottle to test how much remains. It's not too bad, and I drop to an easy stroll, looking ahead.

And after a short distance more, I see what I want: a small clearing.

I stop, rolling my head against neck muscles tight with fatigue then, heaving muggy air, shrug off the backpack once more and set the rifle against a tree-trunk. Unpacking, I find a couple more likely-looking trees, then sling my hammock between two trunks and drape over the mosquito net.

Night falls with the swiftness of the tropics. I sit by my small stove, sipping coffee from the tin mug. With the water boiling again, I tip in my pre-made mix of rice, dehydrated vegetables, dried fish. Humming to myself, I stir the can, then lean back against the trunk again to drink my coffee.

In the leaf litter, a beetle trundles by; a good couple of inches long, maybe more, it's an iridescent green, like some fantastic jewel. No gem I know could compete with this small armoured tank of an insect.

Amazing...

It's an engaging sight, but I don't try to touch the beastie. For anyone interested in such things there's a lifetime's work documenting the small life around here. Personally, I prefer to keep my distance. Insects have some odd defence mechanisms and I'm a long way from any chance of a jab against blood poisoning or anaphylactic shock.

So instead, I watch the shimmering sapphire-emerald little creature struggle through moss and leaves, then with a buzz, launch itself upwards and whirr away, a blue-green ripple in the night until, as it leaves the small circle of light cast by my lamp, it vanishes.

Green eyes...
Wonder what's she's doing now?
What would she think of that waterfall?
Then I chuckle.
She'd probably reach for her paintbrush...
...
Stay focussed...

Taking the rifle down from its place propped against the tree, methodically I check it over. A smooth pull on the trigger and clicks nicely. But it does no harm to be careful and I wipe away a little grit with the oiled rag I keep packed.

The workman and his tools.

*****

TARGET

Dawn finds me already awake, dressed, and rolling hammock and mosquito net into the pack. Standing, limbering up stiff muscles, I drink more coffee and some rewarmed soup

Then rucksack and rifle back in place, I set off to take the short walk to my destination.

*****

I don't need my phone anymore. I've found what I was looking for. Setting down pack and rifle, I pace, examining the ground, choosing my angle.

Way down, perhaps only a mile and a half as the crow flies, sits a fortress.

To the casual eye, I daresay it doesn't *look* like a fortress. This confection of sculpture and architecture could be the grand pleasure palace of any of the super-rich. Set to impress, extravagant gardens stretch all around a central building, all arches, balconies and walkways, set to catch whatever breeze might be there to be had...

Opulent...
Luxurious...
Pretentious...

... but to my eye, knowing my target, it has more the look of a military compound.

Lush greenery; lawn, palms and tropical shrubbery, are the setting for a central swimming pool, edged by terracing set out with loungers, some occupied. There's a smaller dip-pool, tables and seating.

But the gardens are surrounded by a wall. To the front entrance, the wall is painted white and oh-so-attractive, but solidly built and a good twenty feet high. Guards patrol a walkway at the top.

The grounds run down to the sea and moorings where a yacht sits bobbing on the waves.

Behind the house are the kinds of utilitarian building you might expect in a place of this sort: garages, workrooms and suchlike. But also, away from prying eyes, is the compound.

Outwardly, also white-painted, it looks elegant and in keeping with the villa. To any observer standing outside, it would appear a simple extension of the main gardens. Not that any observer would be able to see inside through the solidly built structure.

Who would know, what was in there?

Unless they *looked*.

In these days of satellite photography and the gradual mapping of the world... I smile to myself. It was so *easy* to find all this...

... once I looked.

Ain't the internet marvellous?

The neat driveway to the main house splits to a side-track, leading to the compound gates: as tall as the containing wall, solid and barred. In the centre of the compound a building squats; block-built, small barred windows, solid roof. The single door I can see is sheet steel with a slot window, double drop-bars and locked with a heavy-duty padlock.

Cellblock?

There's no sign of anything resembling air-conditioning or fans. To one side, a couple of buckets sit by what might be a standpipe.

But nothing much is happening. The sole guard patrols, more or less. Mainly, he slouches in the shade of the building.

I check the angle of the sun, gauging by eye whether I'm safe to...

Reflections from glass...

Yes.

I choose my spot to lie; on bare rock and hopefully to avoid being targeted as a meal by the various crawlers I notice at ground level. At arm's length and with the edge of my knife, I flick away a couple of choice specimens.

One with yellow and black stripes, some version of a wasp, or maybe an ant, suggests a critter that is able to stand up for itself. I let it make its own way in the other direction before I lie down. Another, with more legs than I'm comfortable with, is sent on its way over the rock edge.

Then lying flat on my stomach, tucked behind a small, shrubby something-or-other, I raise binoculars, scanning the area.

Several women already lie out by the pool, working on their tans. All are glamorous in a Hollywood starlet kind of way. Tall, leggy, busty: they could, every one, be the lead in some back-street porn movie. None wears more than a thong. Several wear less.

Scanning over the women again, examining their faces...

Anyone I know...?

... that I might have sent here?

I scan each blandly beautiful face with their designer make-up and designer bodies...

None are familiar...

... and I pass over.

...

Great green eyes, in alabaster skin set in a sea of copper-red hair...

Get a grip...

...

Armed figures patrol the shore and the moorings. More figures stand by the gates, also armed...

What are they carrying?

Some kind of semi-automatic rifle...

Or are they SMGs?

It hardly matters. Nothing they have is remotely capable of the range needed to hit me, even if they knew where to aim.

I look back to my own rifle; a TAC-50, a sniper's weapon; which I chose, for this specific occasion, for its reputation for extreme distance sharp-shooting. The round is capable of piercing light armour. It's anyone's guess what it will do to a human body.

In fact, I tested that, while I was trying out the weapon, on a pig carcass. At the shorter range I used, the carcass more or less vanished save for a red haze. At this distance...

A TAC-50 brought down an ISIS terrorist at over two miles. And my target won't be at anything *like* that range. Perhaps a little over half the distance...

When he appears...

It's getting hot again, but without the heavy exertion of the previous day, I'm much more comfortable... probably more than can be said for anyone inside the compound building.

About mid-morning, another guard, gun in hand, joins the first, unlocks the cell block and a dozen or so figures, all female, trudge out.

Sunlight glints on the metal cuffs at ankle and wrist. All the women are young and attractive, or would be, cleaned up and in decent clothes. As it is, black, white and every shade in between, they're all in rags...

The women walk a couple of weary circles around the compound, shielding their eyes against the sun. One of the guards barks something at them and they stand to queue by the stand-pipe, taking turns to run water into the buckets, splash it over their faces and arms.

The last two of the women to wash refill the buckets then, with the others, at the end of the gun, trudge back inside, carrying the water with them. One of the guard re-locks the door behind them, then the pair saunter into the shade to smoke again.

And I settle to resume my vigil.

*****

James – Thirty-Seven weeks

The wee small hours. A full moon slants across the floor, painting the room in weird monochromatic shades, painting everything in shades of light and dark.

Michael lies in his accustomed position on the far side of the bed, his back to me but his ribs moving with the smooth rise and fall of sleep.

Between us lies Charlotte, and I lie spooned around her, her spine pressed against my chest, and my arm curving around her so I can rest a hand over her distended belly.

Every so often, there's movement against my fingers from inside my sleeping love; a foot or an elbow, pushing at me and I smile to myself as my unborn daughter parties through the night.

Charlotte sighs and shifts, the rhythm of her breathing changing.

Is she asleep?

Keeping my voice low, "You alright?"

"I'm fine, Master." She sounds a little sleepy, but not just that. Something else lurks there.

I nuzzle into her hair to kiss the back of her neck. "You sure of that?"

She's silent; too long silent.

"Charlotte? If something's wrong, tell me. Are you feeling ill?"

"No. No nothing like that, Master."

"What then? There's something."

She speaks slowly. "I suppose I'm missing how it was. Before..." She moves her hand over mine... "Before I was pregnant,"

"Missing what? Has so much changed?"

"The fun we used to have *downstairs*. Sometimes it feels as though we're never going to *play* again. You know, just enjoying ourselves. Being *us*. The three of us."

"If you imagine, Milady, that I am going to string my eight-month pregnant wife up by the wrists on a St Andrew's Cross and flog her within an inch of her life, you are very much mistaken. After Cara is born, that's different, but *right now*..."

She chuckles. "I know, Master. But I *do* miss it and... Well, the two of you don't seem *interested* anymore."

"Michael, are you awake? Are you hearing this?"

He rolls over to face me, propping himself up on an elbow. "I'm hearing it."

"And?"

"And I've never heard anything so damn silly. Charlotte, much as I'd love to bend you over the end of the bed, or the couch, or the kitchen table three times a day and poke out your brains, it's not appropriate right now." Irritation wars with sympathy in his voice. "And I'm quite sure James feels the same way."

Not like Michael...

Maybe he's feeling the strain of his 'restraint'...

But the shiver in her spine trembles through my breastbone...

Really upset...

And not wanting to say so...

Have we overdone it?

... and my gaze meets his, a glint of white in the moonlit darkness.

He slow-blinks, palming her cheek. "Charlotte, *truly*. I want nothing more than to make love *with* you, and *to* you; just you and me, with James, with Beth and Richard, *whatever*... forever and always. I... James and I... simply wanted to take the pressure off you."

She's rigid against me, listening closely as he continues... "It's not every woman who's cut out to handle two - let's face it - pretty highly-charged men in her life, even in normal times... And with the best will in the world, you *have* been tired recently. Understandably so. James and I discussed this. We were just trying to show a little consideration... Give you a break."

"Really?"
"Yes, *really*... James?"
How could we have missed this?
I curve around her to kiss her ear. "Charlotte..." She sighs, starting to roll... "*No,* stay on your side. Let us do the work. Stay comfortable but lift your leg."

As she raises a knee, Michael pulls away a pillow from under his head, pushing it between her knees, then pulls closer to her.

My cock rises all unbidden, hardening by the moment

Pressing myself against her, pressing my burgeoning erection against her tailbone, letting her feel me, I slide my hand from belly to breast, stroking and soothing soft skin, but nipping and tugging at her nipples which firm and harden under my touch.

I'm not sure what Michael is doing. His shoulders are moving; from the angle, perhaps he's stroking her thighs, moving in on her bud.

Hooking my hands into the crease of legs to torso, I pull her back towards me and closer, angling her, probing into her. "Let me in, Charlotte."

She exhales, a soft, easy sound, spreading her knees further and Michael shoves in another pillow to support her splayed thighs. I curve around to reach her from the front with my hand, and I reach for her with my cock from the rear.

She's so wet. And so warm.

She's wanted this...

Yes, we've been over-cautious...

She's open, flowing and ready for me. The angle's a little awkward for me, but I guide myself with fingers to first anchor to her entrance then slowly, mindfully, to enter her.

As I penetrate, she whimpers; a *good* sound, full of promise and hope and joy and pleasure. Safely inside, I glide my hand to her breasts and Michael moves in, working her clit. But he's kissing her too. Even from my position behind, I can see his kiss is soft; seducing her, calming her. And he talks; I can't make out his words, but it's a calm, gentle murmur; a stream of reassurance...

Her Lover...

Deep inside her now, I take the time to breathe; long, slow inhalations, then letting the air out slowly, I take command of myself, resisting the urge to plunge, thrust a couple of times and shoot.

My beautiful Jade-Eyes...
We tried to protect you... Against ourselves...
And all we have done is rob our Triad of its continuity.

Sexuality, sensuality, love... whatever you call it. Physical love has been the anchor for our spiritual love right from the beginning. It was a mistake to try to hold back from that.

All we need is to be careful.

I rest my face by hers. "Are you comfortable, Charlotte? Supported where you need it?"

"Yes, Master. It's... wonderful."

I kiss her cheek. "Good. If at any point you are *not* comfortable, say so."

"Yes, Master."

A finger under her chin, Michael tilts her face to his. "You *will* say so, won't you?" He brushes his lips over hers. "If it's not working, for whatever reason, you must tell us and we'll figure another way of doing things. Okay?"

She nods. "Yes, okay."

I enfold her in my arms; one at the crease of belly to thigh, the other below her breasts, pulling her in close, *so* close, as I begin to move.

The angle makes it easy for me to catch her sweet spot, targeting her inside and drawing moans with every long, slow thrust. Michael, open-mouthed, one hand around the back of her head, is kissing her; the other hand tormenting her clit.

Soft moans rumble through her, echoing through my chest as, her skin and mine both slick with sweat, I slide past her as I slow-fuck her.

Her heart is pounding, accelerating; thumping through to my arm where I have captured her at the ribs. And inside, she's heating, tightening, beginning to pulse.

She smells hot and heady, sweat running through her hair, slicking her shoulders and spine. The scent is musky, a counterpoint to the perfume from her sex; pungent, intoxicating and, for me, addictive.

For me, she is my drug. I couldn't give her up if I wanted to.

And I don't want to.

Her body is *thrumming*...

And as she bucks and moans, shuddering back against me, I surrender and spill into my Jade-Eyed Love.

*****

Michael – Thirty-Eight Weeks

Charlotte waddles into the lounge. And it's a slow waddle. Her feet drag and her breathing's heavy, her face flushed.
I stand, offering my arm to help her sit. "You okay, Babe?"
"I suppose." She reaches around herself, trying to rub at the small of her back. "I'm so tired all the time. And so *hot*..."
Just as well it's winter...
"... And my back's hurting." She's drooping almost as I watch.
I follow her hand with mine to the base of her spine, feeling for the pressure-point; where's she's tense. "Why don't I give you a massage? Let's see if we can ease this up for you a bit."
"That would be nice."
I slide my arm under hers, trying to help her back up again. She heaves upwards, then drops back. So instead, I stand, this time giving her both hands to haul her onto her feet. "C'mon, let's get you upstairs onto the bed and I'll see what I can do."

*****

On the bed, she's so quiet. Lying on her side, her back turned to me, head on a pillow, her hands rest by her face.
"Would you like a pillow to your front? Or between your knees?"
"Mmm..." She nods sleepily.
Was that a yes to one or the other or both?
But she's drifting and I don't want to disturb her, so I give her both, lifting her leg to push one between her knees and another under 'Bump'.
My oil is pre-prepared. I thought this would come and I've made sure to keep what I need on hand. Almond base with a little lavender and chamomile, to help to calm her, relax her.
My position on the bed is a little awkward. It's a bit low and I'm having to twist as I sit beside her. I would have preferred to have her on

a proper table, but I don't want to ask her to walk to the hotel. As for comfort, which of us is more uncomfortable?

Long smooth strokes...

Up and along... either side of her spine... Her muscles are knotted tight.

Ah... you're hurting, Babe...

Taking my time, I smooth the tension away. "That good?"

Drowsily, "Mmm, yes."

"I'm not hurting you at all?"

A slow shake of the head. "No."

Her belly ripples and she hisses.

"Another one?"

"Yes." She robs over her stomach. I don't think it's the real thing yet, but..."

"How does it feel?"

"Sort of crampy."

I thumb over her shoulders. "I know it must be uncomfortable, but it's right on target. You can expect to get these intermittent contractions over the next few days. It's your body softening up your cervix for real labour."

She groans; quietly, softly. "How will I know when it's real labour?"

"Instead of being one-offs that die away, they'll keep getting stronger. Don't worry. I've got your hospital bag packed and ready. And one for Cara too. Just have a think about if there's anything else you would like in there."

She reaches behind herself, takes my hand and squeezes. "My Golden Lover. You're always there aren't you. Knowing what's needed."

I squeeze back. "I know James is the one going to the clinic with you, but I've been doing quite a bit of reading myself. And I talked with some of the staff. A couple of them have a nursing background. And your mother too. So I know what to expect."

"Is he happy? With how it's going?"

"Who? James? He's walking on sunshine. I don't think there is anything you could have done that would have made him happier than this. What makes you ask?"

"He's my Master but your friend. You see a different side of him to me."

I glide palms over the length of her. "Where's your back hurting?"

"Lower down."

Shifting down, "There?"

"Lower. Base of my spine."

I press the heel of my hand over her coccyx, circling, easing the pressure away. "That helping?"

"Yes, it is. It's lovely."

A movement at the door: James. He hovers there for a moment, watching me with our naked, pregnant, exhausted beauty. His eyes are soft, and he blinks a little, then moves to the other side of the bed to sit beside her.

She shifts a little as he joins her, looking up to his face. "Sorry, Master. I'm just so tired. I never expected it to be this hard, but it is."

James strokes her swollen belly, then takes her hand, kissing the fingers before replacing it on the pillow. "Hardly surprising. Just a few more days and you can introduce us all to Cara, then you can get back to feeling more yourself."

"There's the labour first. I'm... I'm not looking forward to that."

He takes the hand again, this time holding it in his. "Almost every woman goes through it. *Everything* and *everyone* will be there to be sure it all goes as it should for both of you."

She shifts, half turning, trying to face both of us. "You're sure it's better in a hospital? I'd really like..."

James' voice turns a little firmer. "If you really insist, I'll arrange for you to birth at home, but for your first, I would be much happier if you were in a hospital. Just in case." He eyes me in a very obvious and intended cue. "What do *you* think, Michael?"

"I agree. I'd prefer you to be in a hospital too, this time round. And if, as we all expect, everything goes smoothly, then you can do it at home next time."

I expect her to argue, but she doesn't, simply sighing and nodding.

Then she jolts under my touch. "You *will* both be there won't you?" She grows insistent, a panicky edge to her voice. "*Both* of you."

James meets my eye over her but stages a chuckle. "*Yes*, we'll both be there. You don't pay for private health care to have midwives argue over something like that."

She eases again, relaxing back to my touch. "Good. That's alright then. If you're both there, I know everything will be fine."

James regards her for a long moment, lips pursing. "Tell you what," he says. "We'll be at the hospital for your check-up tomorrow. I'll be taking you, of course. But afterwards, we could go out. Somewhere nice, a restaurant, Francesca's. Anywhere you like."

"That sounds nice, Master." I can't see her face, but now I hear the smile in her voice.

"Where would you like to go?"

"Anywhere, you choose." Her head twists as she tries to look back to me, but her body doesn't move with her and I still only have a side view. "Will you come too?"

"'Course I will. What time's your appointment?"

James turns brisk. "We should be done by two. You can meet us at the hospital."

*****

Klempner - Thailand

And in the heat of the afternoon...
Movement. By the main entrance of the villa...
Ahhh....
There he is...
Garcias...
White-suited, he strolls from the house, surrounded by...
By what?
Again, I don't know the faces, the individuals; but the body language is there... Fawning, bowing; subtly, and not so subtly; they defer to this man, who from the look of him, is barking orders.
There's a woman with him, tall, willowy, blonde, dressed in an ornate, overly-elaborate white dress that shrieks of more money than taste.
The same woman I saw him with before?
Or just a 'clone'?
His type...
I'm not sure. But her body language, similar to the woman at the hotel, is interesting. Despite the expensive clothes and the sparkle at neck and wrist, she walks no closer to Garcias than is strictly necessary.
Not a partner or a wife then.
An ornament.
Garcias strolls the gardens, following footpaths laid out in quads and circles, apparently taking the air. Several times he disappears from view, behind a tree or in the shadow of the perimeter wall.
It's not going to be an easy shot.
One chance only.
And I watch.
He takes a seat at the poolside, gesturing to the woman and she snaps to the seat next to him, arranging herself *just so*; legs crossed at the ankles, hands clasped.

Scared...
A slave with privileges...
A servant serves from a jug into tall glasses. Again, visibly cringing, head ducking down, she pours...

... and stumbles, splashing bright orange juice over Garcias' woman and the fancy gown.

Garcias stands, backhanding her to the ground, shouting incoherently, first at her, then to the guards, gesticulating to the rear compound.

The girl is weeping and pleading, grovelling at his feet, but two of the guards take her, one to each arm, lifting her and dragging her to the compound.

Garcias spins on 'his' woman, as though she's about to get it too, but there's a call from the doorway, some minion waving an arm and holding up a phone.

Garcias yells something back, then with a jerk, stalks to the house, snatches the handset away and vanishes inside. The blonde takes her cue from his disappearance and scuttles off to join the rest of the sunbathers.

The sun's getting high and the angle could betray me with reflections, so I put the binoculars away. Taking my time, I pace up and down, squinting against the light as I consider where to set up.

One chance...

In the heat of the day, all grows still, with only the susurration of insects for sound. Even the birds fall silent.

Then, in the distance, but growing louder, the sound of an engine. It rumbles closer, the sound dropping an octave as it crunches into a lower gear. A truck grinds up the drive. More guards open the main gates then close them again as the truck follows the track to the rear. Now the compound gates swing open, then close again as it parks up.

In the still air, the guards' voices carry. Not that I can pick out the words, even if I understood Thai, but the harsh bullying tone comes through perfectly as twenty or more women step down from the back of the truck, to stand, heads hanging. Some are crying. Others simply stand, arms wrapped around themselves.

As the sun falls, the door opens and Garcias reappears, shouting something, his arms waving.

Perfect timing...

I stand, stroll around a bit, limber up...

The adrenaline is pounding.

Calm down...

I hold out my hand. It's trembling a little.

I stroll some more, take a couple of deep breaths, then try again, splaying fingers.

Steady as a rock...

Taking my place, flat-chested to the ground, I sight him.

The crosshairs weave one way then the other until...

There... Got him...

... they centre squarely over my target.

It's a hell of a shot.

Over a mile

It's been done before...

I'm not quite comfortable, the ground uneven under my ribs, so I shift the biped a little.

That's better...

I inhale the sweet perfume of earth and rotting vegetation, mixed with the scent of gun oil. The birds are louder somehow. The buzz of insects more intense.

Focus on the *right* senses

Concentrate...

There's a breeze up here, but down *there* I can't see even a whisper of movement in the palm fronds.

Head shot or chest?

Chest...

More reliable at this range.

Two figures emerge from the villa, moving to stand beside him. One of the men is blond, the other dark. Wearing normal civilian clothes, they look to be arguing about something.

Who are they?
His sons?
Bodyguards?
Not in those clothes.
Does it matter?
Probably not.

And I squeeze the trigger.

So far to travel, even a bullet takes a few seconds reach its target...

Time *stretches*... as I wait...

Plaster spits on the wall behind Garcias. Only off by a few inches, but it's still a miss.

Fuck!

All three dive, necks craned to see where the shot came from, but I'm already aiming again for Garcias.

One of the 'sons', the blond, pushes Garcias off-side. I fire again...

One... Two... Three...

... and the blond's chest splashes red, spattering Garcias.

My heart pounds hard enough to shudder up my arm as I move. The snap and click of the rifle bolt is a smooth, almost poetic motion as I aim once more.

Garcias is running now, pelting for the shelter of the villa. But I'm targeting again, now not at him, but at where he's *going* to be in... six... five... four...

I *fire*...

... and inhale... three... two... *one*... seconds.

... and as I exhale again, he falls, mouth flung wide as his white suit erupts into blood

The sunbathers are screaming, women running for cover in all directions, some clutching towels to their breasts as they flee, others simply dashing for cover. The guards aren't much better; an ants' nest of panicky activity as they too sprint for cover, some looking wildly out as they try to figure where the shots came from.

I've two rounds left in the magazine and I use them in quick succession, missing my target with the first, but downing another guard with the second.

But as he falls, another sees, looking out and towards me, flinging out an arm and yelling. Another close by snatches a handset from his pocket, yammering into it.

Time to *leave*...

I snap the legs of the bipod back into place. Then standing, shrug on my backpack, sling the rifle over my shoulder and step smartly out on my planned escape route: not the way I came in, in case anyone picks up my tracks, but a continuation of my 'pig-track', along the ridge and, eventually, to the harbour.

With barely a hundred yard behind me, I hear the *thwack, thwack, thwack* of...

Fuck...

A helicopter rises from somewhere beyond the house...

Where the fuck did that come from?

*And **why** didn't I see the pad in the satellite shots?*

?

?

Out of date images?

The 'copter rises, swinging up and circling over the complex before the remaining 'son' runs out, yelling upwards and gesticulating in my direction.

Crap!

Stepping up my pace, I march, trying to watch both my footing and the 'copter headed my way...

What model?
No tail rotor...
KA-50?
Oh, fucking ***brilliant****...*
Expensive toy for a crime baron...
Police in his pocket?
??
What does it come with?
Trying to run and think at the same time I dredge my out-dated knowledge of air-mounted artillery and the vehicles that carry it...
30mm cannon...
High frag? AP? Incendiary?
Semi-rigid mounting though...
So, he can't turn too much to aim...
How much?
No idea...
...

What to *do?*
??
Run for it...?
Hide 'til nightfall, then run...?
??
Equipped with infra-red?
Probably.
No point waiting for sundown then.
Better to stand and fight now...
... while the heat of the day works for me...
Where?
??
The forest...
Some cover at least...
...

How far was it?
All uphill... not as far as it felt...
The chopper circles, then slants off, following the trail.
Spotted the track from the air?
But not me...
Yet...
The *chop chop* of the rotors abruptly cuts off as it rounds the ridge and disappears from sight.
Carpe diem...
How long? Before it's back...
Ten minutes?
Five?
Two?
Run...
U-turning, I set off at as fast a jog as I can manage for the cover of the forest...
Get rid of some weight...
Shrugging off the backpack, I take out the spare mags - stashing them into a back pocket – and the water bottle, then shove the pack over the edge of the cliff-face. Then, shouldering the rifle once more, I go...
Sprinting hard back the way I came, downhill all the way, not bothering with cover while the copter's out of sight, I make good progress. Freed of the weight of the pack, and with the gradient working for me now, just now the main danger is a stumble...
A twisted ankle...
It would finish me.
Prudence says I need to slow down, watch my feet, but now from behind, the sound again of rotors, closer, louder...
And I'm exposed here, with no tree cover; the naked track against a naked rock face and me... in plain view...

Loose stones skitter under my boots as I take one giant bound then another, leaping across ground that should be carefully negotiated.

And now, behind and above me, the roar of engines, the whoosh of air and...

The ground explodes into splintered rock in a racing line beside me as I run. A hundred yards more and the forest will close over me... Something slashes into my shoulder.

Pain...

But fuelled by adrenaline and terror, the pain is... nothing. After a moment it fades...

And the forest, the blessed green canopy draws closer.

Another line of fire shatters the rotted carcass of some forest giant; rotted wood bursts in all directions, showering me in God-knows-what, but the treeline is right ahead of me and with a scream of tortured engines, the coptor swings up, clear the trees and away into clear air.

And I pelt into shaded green safety...

More or less...

Above me, above the canopy, a shadow hovers, a dark silhouette. Dodging between one tree and the next, I stay covered as best I can, but the shadow follows...

Infra-red...

...

Infra-red...

The waterfall...

The overhang...

I move quickly, darting from tree-trunk to tree-trunk, pausing to gather my breath behind one before sprinting for the next. Over the clatter of the rotors, the roar of water grows louder.

And ahead me, the forest opens once more to the roaring falls.

I don't bother to admire the view. There's no shelter between me and my target. Above me, the shadow screams forward, then swings through one-eighty to bear on me as, dashing headlong for the overhang I leap from one slick stepping-stone to another.

Sheer momentum keeps me upright as, helter-skelter I dash for cover trying, impossibly, to outrun the gunfire which chatters and screams behind me, biting at my footsteps.

Skidding, I leap first one way, then another as a single rock, then a line of rocks squeals and shatters by my feet. Doubled-over as I run, I almost lose my footing and, at the last moment, regain my balance as moss, green gunk and ferns explode in a running line off the slick rock-face.

Full pelt, I vault headlong through the curtain of water and under the shelter of the overhang.

My mind skitters and veers in excited panic, but my body reacts by rote, doing its thinking all independent of my brain, letting training and adrenaline work their magic.

Ignoring the pounding of my heart, the rasping of my lungs and taking orders directly from the base of my spine, my hands swing the rifle from my shoulder and to the ground, snap in a fresh magazine...

My body follows, and with a few seconds respite, my brain regroups.

The water curtain flows and ripples and shimmers all but continuously. Here, the infra-red won't penetrate, and I cannot be betrayed by my own body-heat.

But in a few spots, the curtain parts; inches only, and with wayward splashes and ripples, but the narrow openings are there; enough to poke the muzzle of my rifle through and to aim.

The copter hangs above, meandering in the air above, slightly concealed by the line of the canopy edge, but nonetheless, silhouetted against bright blue sky...

Idiots...

... a perfect target...

Range?

A couple of hundred feet?
Less...
The angle's more difficult than the range. As the thing hovers and swings, a grey vulture over the trees, I stack flattish rocks under the biped, twisting to look, trying to bear on the damn thing, then lying flat-shouldered to the ground, I squint upwards to sight...
Where are the fucking fuel tanks?
Does it matter? At this range?
Modern copters...
No space unoccupied these days. Bound to hit something vital.
Go for it.
Nudging the sights first one way, then as it shifts, the other, I aim, square-on for the front windscreen and the shadow of the pilot behind it.
Finger around the trigger... I squeeze...
Fuck!
... then roll to one side as the recoil just about dislocates my shoulder at the ridiculous angle I'm lying...
But the pain vanishes under a haze of euphoria as, above me, flame blooms and belatedly, I slap palms over my ears, curling in on myself...
The shock wave ricochets over me, making the water curtain shiver and my ear-drums bang. The rush of falling water competes with the *glock-glock-glock* of falling metal, whirling to destruction, before with a sound that crashes over me, what remains of the chopper meets the ground and...
I start up sit up to look, then my brain takes over from my tourist instincts...
This isn't the moment to sit up and admire your handiwork...
The pressure wave *thumps* against my chest, drawing out the air, winding me. With an effort, I bang my ribs with a fist, knocking the air back in then, scrambling up, hefting the rifle back onto my shoulder, I abandon my watery shelter and *run...*

Where to?
??
Does this change anything?
No...
Time to vanish then...
Back to the city crowds...

*****

James - Thirty-Nine Weeks

The nurse is brisk, speaking from a view between Charlotte's knees. "Everything is fine. The baby has turned and is now in the correct position for delivery. And..." She nods down to Charlotte's 'dropped' abdomen, "... you can see for yourself that she is moving down. You're a textbook case, Mrs Summerford."

I squeeze Charlotte's hand and the nurse sits upright. "Your cervix is at half an inch, but that's not a very reliable sign of anything, especially for your first. What I would say is..."

She swings to me, her attention moving between my face and the space between Charlotte's knees. "... Have the hospital bag packed and you..." She levels a finger at me... "...make sure you have petrol in your tank. When you're sure she's in full labour, bring her in."

"Of course. Thank you, nurse."

She lays a hand on my arm. "*Everything* is absolutely normal, Mr Summerford. Exactly what we'd expect at this stage. Don't you worry about anything. Your wife's in good hands."

"I'm sure of that. Thank you."

Charlotte struggles to sit up. "I need to pee."

I help her upright, then as she struggles to reach, slip her white cotton panties over her ankles and tug them up for her. She lurches off the gyne table, totters while, my hand cupping her elbow, she catches her balance, then tugs them up the rest of the way.

"I'll bet you're looking forward to not having to say that every five minutes."

"You bet." She strokes the white hospital gown smooth over herself, trying to pull it enough together to protect her modesty. Still it flaps loose.

I've seen it before Green-Eyes...

"Should I come with you?"

Injecting dignity into her voice, "I can make it to the bathrooms by myself thank you." I keep my face straight.

"Want me to help you get dressed properly?"

"I'll manage, thank you."

"Let me just close you up back here..."

I follow her out of the room, struggling to close the dreadful gown enough to cover her, to pull the ties tight; but she tugs away, irritable, her voice short. "I've *got* to pee." And she shuffles down the corridor to the bathrooms.

"I'll be in the waiting area then."

She neither replies nor looks back.

Can't cope with needing help...

Always been too self-reliant...

I help myself to a vending machine coffee and take a seat. Women, some alone, some in couples, wait around me.

Thirty years since I last did this...

Just like old times...

And all unbidden, a grin plasters itself over my face. Across the room, some guy, a youngster, a stranger, but sitting with a young woman's hand in his, meets my eyes and answers with a matching grin, rolling his eyes down to her protruding belly.

The coffee is *terrible*. Classic vending machine crap. Surreptitiously, I tip what's left into the pot of a cheese plant, then look for somewhere to dump the cup. In the background somewhere, a siren wails off into the distance.

"Ah, there you are." It's Michael, looming over me. "All done?"

"Yes, she's fine. Everything normal. On the countdown according to the nurse."

"That she is." He beams, head swinging. "Where is she?"

"Making the eternal pilgrimage to the bathroom."

He scratches at an ear. "Should think she'll be glad to finish with that, eh?"

"You took the words from my mouth." I glance at my watch. "She's taking a while. I booked the table for half past. I'll just go give her a knock."

The bathrooms are left along a hall, another left, a right and then along a corridor.

Which idiot came up with that as a design for an ante-natal clinic?

At the women's restroom, I give the door a tap. "Charlotte, Michael's here. Time for us to be heading out."

No response.

I knock again. "Charlotte, everything alright in there?"

Silence.

I try once more. "Charlotte, are you in there?"

Crickets.

A young woman with the matching hospital gown and a strained expression pushes past me.

"Excuse me, could you see if my wife is in there. Redhead. Name of Charlotte."

She gives me a startled glance...

Not many men my age in a place like this...

But, "Yes, of course."

She enters but returns a few seconds later. "No, she's not in here."

??

"You're sure?"

"Sure I'm sure. There's no one else. See for yourself." She swings the door wide, letting me see inside. "'Scuse me." And she teeters to a cubical, her footsteps echoing against blank tiles as the door swings back in my face.

Cracking the door open, "Sorry to bother you again. Is there another Ladies' washroom nearby?"

From the cubical; splashing and a sigh of relief. "Couldn't say. Ask at the desk."

Where the hell is she?

Took a wrong turn on the way back?

I stand, palms held up uselessly, as though I could somehow conjure Charlotte up from the ether that way.

There's nothing *here*.

One bathroom door. One fire-extinguisher mounted on the wall. One emergency exit. One wall poster. *Smoking is forbidden in all parts of this building.*

Just on the off-chance, I lift the bar of the exit, poking my head out. Of course, there's nothing there but a few parking spaces... *Authorised Persons Only.*

I head back, meeting Michael coming around the corner. "Found her?"

"No."

"Well, she can't have gone far. Maybe she used a different bathroom."

"I suppose." I stride smartly back to the waiting area to see if Charlotte somehow worked around me. Again, there's no sign of her, so u-turning, I try the right-hand corridor instead.

Still nothing.

A touch of worry gnaws, somewhere deep.

A porter pushes a trolley by me. "Excuse me, have you seen a young woman? A redhead." I hold my arms out in a 'Humpty-Dumpty' stomach impression. "Very pregnant. I think she might have gotten turned about on herself."

"A redhead? No, sir, I haven't, but I'll ask for you. It happens sometimes. These corridors all look alike if you don't know your way around."

Twenty minutes later, there's still no sign of Charlotte and a full search is underway.

The tannoy blarts: *Would Mrs Summerford please report to the nearest reception desk. This is a call for Mrs Charlotte Summerford...*

Michael, red-faced, looks set to explode.

A doctor taps my arm. "Mr Summerford?" His eyes... Something haunts them...

"I'm the father, yes."

"You'd better come with me, sir."

His skin is shiny, pasty almost, and that maggot of worry in my gut crawls faster.

Michael follows us and the doctor gives him an odd look but doesn't argue when I don't. He leads us to the security office. In the background somewhere, sirens are pulsing closer.

"When you raised concerns as to the whereabouts of your wife... Mr Summerford..." He looks between us, but continues... "...and she wasn't quickly located... I asked the security guard to check the surveillance cameras for the last half hour." He licks his lips, seeming about to baulk. "I've already called the police, but you'd better see this."

The sirens are growing louder.

His hand trembles as he mouses the cursor over a monitor. "There's no sound I'm afraid." He stands clear to let us see the grainy black-and-white image.

Seen from behind, Charlotte, still trying to tug the gown properly closed behind her, waddles along the corridor to the bathroom I found empty. As she vanishes inside, two figures in green porters' overalls push a patient trolley into view between them.

One follows in behind her. The other waits outside, one hand in a pocket, looking back down the corridor, apparently keeping watch.

Seconds later, the door opens again, this time with Charlotte, eyes wide in panic, struggling and trying to scream, being shoved out by the man, one arm locked around her, the other hand clapped over her face.

The one waiting pulls his hand from his pocket, holding a hypodermic. Her eyes widen further, showing whites all around as she sees the needle...

Her captor abruptly curses, releases her, and shaking his hand, spatters blood on the walls, blood reflected over her mouth.

In her bare moment of freedom, Charlotte lashes out with a punch at the one with the needle, simultaneously screaming down the corridor.

There's no sound, but I can *see* her screamed plea for help, her face distorting as she cries out.

"*Mast...*"

... before her cry is cut off as he backhands her then drives the needle deep to her arm and presses the plunger home.

Within seconds, her head droops and she falls. The two catch her, laying her limp and unmoving on the trolley and covering her to the neck with a blanket. Then, banging up the bar of the emergency exit door, they wheel the trolley out, taking my unconscious Charlotte with them.

*****

The Story will Continue in 'Ransom'

Free Audiobook
'Friends'
'Mastering the Virgin' Part One

The Boys are Back in Town....

James is a Dom. Michael loves women.
When the two become unlikely friends, they form a team, working the clubs and enjoying a carefree bachelor existence.
Until, one day, James is offered an unusual opportunity: to Buy A Virgin...
The First Part In A Tale of BDSM, Ménage Erotic Romance.

---

1. https://www.simone-leigh.com/books/friends-mastering-the-virgin-1-audiobook/

CLAIM 'FRIENDS'
THE AUDIOBOOK [2]

2. https://payhip.com/b/XDHE

'Her Master's Wedding' 'Charlotte's Search' Part One
FREE DOWNLOAD

When you Marry Two Men What Happens Next?

As Charlotte's wedding day approaches, will her marriage to one of her Masters affect her relationship with the other?

Has her old enemy forgotten her? And will the past return to reveal its secrets?

A BDSM Ménage Romance and Thriller

---

3. https://books2read.com/her-masters-wedding

[DOWNLOAD 'HER MASTER'S WEDDING'][4]

---

[4] https://books2read.com/her-masters-wedding

'Mastering the Virgin' Box Set One
FREE DOWNLOAD

You've read 'Buying the Virgin'? Told from Charlotte's point of view? Now read 'Mastering the Virgin', where James and Michael get their say.

The Boys are Back in Town....
Two Friends
One Virgin
One Week
It was all supposed to be about sex – a bit of fun.

---

5. https://books2read.com/mastering-virgin-box-set-one

No-one mentioned Love....
A BDSM, Ménage Erotic Romance

'Triad'
'Mastering the Virgin' Part Thirteen
FREE DOWNLOAD

The Past Returns....
She sold herself, and then she returned to him, her Master, and to her Lover
Now, the Three believe her past is behind her.
But Dark Forces are moving....
A BDSM Ménage Erotic Thriller

7. https://books2read.com/triad

[DOWNLOAD 'TRIAD'][8]

---

8. https://books2read.com/triad

See The Book Trailer
'Mastering the Virgin' Box Set Three

9

10

---

9. https://youtu.be/jECgJ4V8OJ0

10. https://youtu.be/jECgJ4V8OJ0

See The Book Trailer 'Triad'

11

12

---

11. https://youtu.be/VNvBbVujTCE
12. https://youtu.be/VNvBbVujTCE

Suggested Reading Order For the 'Buying the Virgin' Story

The story of 'Buying the Virgin' started out as a simple little story of a week of auction erotica frolics told from the point of view of Charlotte 'The Virgin', with James, her purchaser and Master, and his friend Michael. This was five episodes making up what is now 'Buying the Virgin' Box Set One

The tale has however, grown in the telling and has expanded to Four Box Sets (with more coming) of 'Buying the Virgin' (BTV), the current four Box Sets of 'Mastering the Virgin' (MTV), with more coming, new characters introduced in 'Kirstie's Tale' and it has absorbed 'Bought by the Billionaire' whole.

Understandably enough, I am receiving an increasing number of requests for a suggested reading order for the books.

So, I've put together a guide in this blog post[13] It's by no means set in stone. Much of BTV and MTV can be read interchangeably, but for those of you who are perhaps new to the story or who have encountered it half-way through, perhaps with a free download of 'Triad' or similar, here's a suggested reading order for you.

---

13. https://www.simone-leigh.com/suggested-reading-order-for-buying-the-virgin/

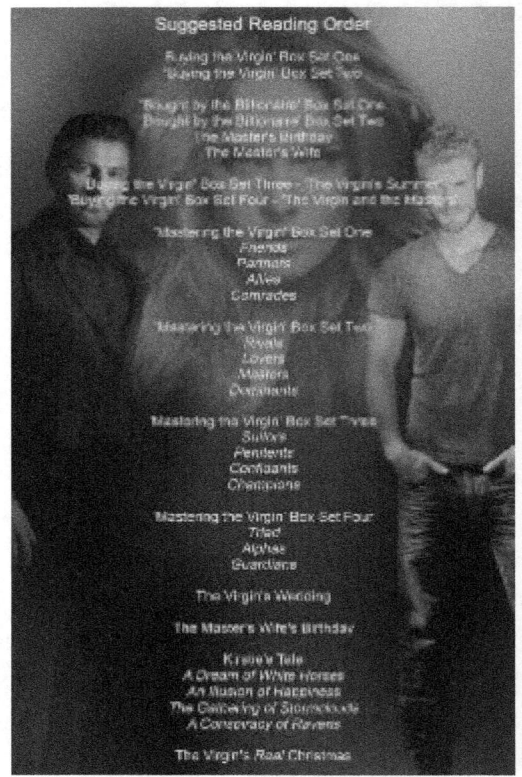

14

15

---

14. https://www.simone-leigh.com/suggested-reading-order-for-buying-the-virgin/

15. https://www.simone-leigh.com/suggested-reading-order-for-buying-the-virgin/

Free Resource
'Buying the Virgin' Timeline Infographic

'Buying the Virgin' started out as a bit of fun erotica. My original intention was to write a series of five short stories that would give readers a 30 minute 'helping' of erotica over a cup of coffee.

But the story has grown in the telling. With four Box Sets out and more to come, side stories, extra characters and.... well.... Spoilers.... Lol!

So far, the tale is up to around 700,000 words and is still growing.

So, for those of you who would like to check in what order to read the books, I have an infographic for you. I update it regularly, and at some point, when I get my 'tech-head' screwed on, I'll produce an improved version with the book links built in.

Hope it helps ?

---

16. http://www.simone-leigh.com/timeline-infographic-for-buying-the-virgin/

[17]

---

17. http://www.simone-leigh.com/timeline-infographic-for-buying-the-virgin/

Free Download
'Red as Blood'
Book One of 'Tales of Blood and Darkness.'
Little Red Riding Hood?

18

Belle is eighteen and should be a woman. Terrified that she may be barren and have no future, she confides in her Grandmother. But as the moon waxes full, she learns that her family has a secret... Darkly erotic re-telling of an old fairy tale.

18. https://www.instafreebie.com/free/2pLV2

164 SIMONE LEIGH

> DOWNLOAD 'RED AS BLOOD' [19]

---

19. https://www.instafreebie.com/free/2pLV2

Want to Read Where It All Started? Free Download "Buying the Virgin. Box Set One"

She Auctioned Herself and Her Virginity

The penniless Charlotte dreams of a bright future, but she has nothing to sell but herself and her virginity. She chooses to auction both to the highest bidder.

What will happen when her owner takes her away?

---
20. https://books2read.com/box-set-1-the-virgin

[21]

---

21. https://books2read.com/box-set-1-the-virgin

Who is Richard Haswell?
Free Download
"Bought by the Billionaire. Box Set One"

Elizabeth is a student working in a dead-end hotel job to makes ends meet, but dreaming of a better life. When she foolishly decides to shower in the penthouse bathroom of one of the hotel guests, it has consequences she did not expect.

A BDSM Billionaire Erotic Romance

---

22. https://books2read.com/bought-by-the-billionaire-box-1

23. https://books2read.com/bought-by-the-billionaire-box-1

Free Download
'Enslaved'
Book One of 'Submissive to Her Master.'
Dying of Boredom?

What has She to Live for?

Martha is jaded with life to the point of suicide. About to end it all, she encounters a stranger who takes her on a wild ride of passion, convincing her that she has something to live for.

'Submissive to Her Master' is a story of Master and Slave, BDSM erotica.

---

24. https://books2read.com/enslaved-submissive-to-her-master

25. https://books2read.com/enslaved-submissive-to-her-master

Free Download
'Freedom'
Book One of 'Call of the Wild.'
A Perfect Life?

26

Anna is a writer, making her living on the move and living her life as free as a bird.

---

26. https://books2read.com/freedom-callofthewild

TARGET 171

She seems to have complete freedom and a perfect life. But is everything as it appears?

[DOWNLOAD 'FREEDOM'][27]

---

27. https://books2read.com/freedom-callofthewild

About the Author

Simone Leigh is English but has lived in Spain for the last few years. Here, she divides her time between working on her tan, renovating her beautiful villa, writing erotica and swimming naked in her swimming pool.

Visit Simone Leigh's Website[28]

http://www.simone-leigh.com/

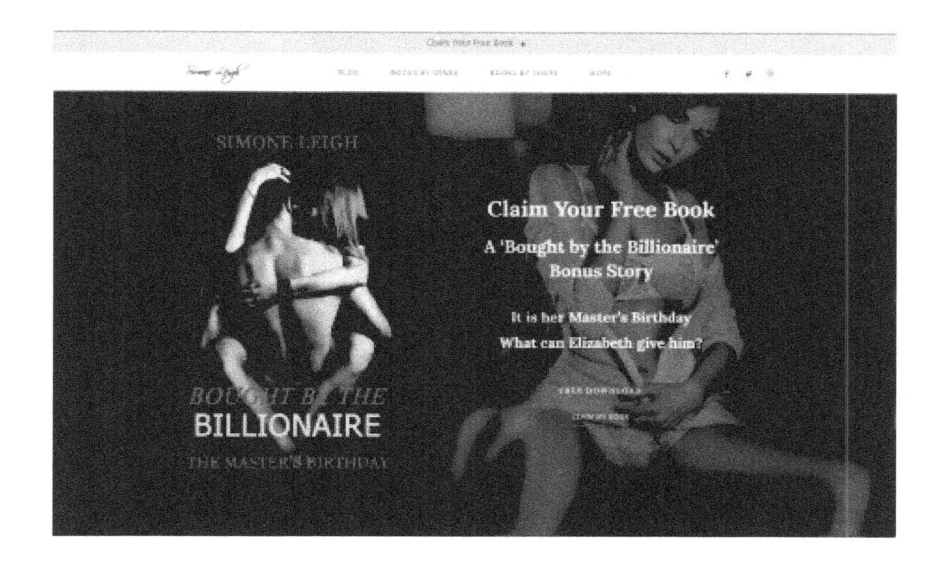

Romantic, Intelligent, Erotic Fiction

---

28. http://www.simone-leigh.com/
29. http://www.simone-leigh.com/

Contact Me

Simone Leigh

If you would like to get in contact, with comments, questions, reviews or even requests the kinds of stories you would like to read in the future, I'd love to hear from you.

Follow Me

Website: https://www.simone-leigh.com/
Facebook page: https://www.facebook.com/perfumepetalsandthorns
YouTube: https://www.youtube.com/channel/UCLa1RTmTBXwOKCxRb-WU69Q
Twitter: https://twitter.com/SimoneLeigh_CBE
Instagram: https://www.instagram.com/simoneleighauthor/
Newsletter Sign-Up: https://www.simone-leigh.com/my-newsletter/
Bookbub: https://www.bookbub.com/profile/simone-leigh
GoodReads: https://www.goodreads.com/author/show/15454039.Simone_Leigh
BookSprout: https://booksprout.co/author/2791/simone-leigh

My Newsletter

If you would like to receive my newsletter, you can click the link below to subscribe. I send it out, typically once a week on Fridays. In it you will get news, offers, free books, competitions and sweepstakes, and my random musings direct to your inbox. And I'll also send you a free book as a welcome gift.

If you would like to see a sample newsletter, you can click the button below to see a recent example.

And of course, you can unsubscribe at any time.

SHOW ME A SAMPLE NEWSLETTER [30]

SIGN ME UP TO THE NEWSLETTER [31]

---

30. https://preview.mailerlite.com/y8i2p3
31. https://www.simone-leigh.com/my-newsletter/

Don't miss out!

Visit the website below and you can sign up to receive emails whenever Simone Leigh publishes a new book. There's no charge and no obligation.

https://books2read.com/r/B-A-AXDD-OPNAB

BOOKS 2 READ

Connecting independent readers to independent writers.

Did you love *Target*? Then you should read *Mastering the Virgin - Box Set One* by Simone Leigh!

The Boys are Back in Town....
Two friends...
One virgin...
One week...
It was all supposed to be about sex...
A bit of fun...
No-one *mentioned* love...
A Tale of BDSM, Ménage Erotic Romance.
Explicit adult content. For mature readers only
This Box Set contains the following stories, previously published separately:
Part One: Friends
Part Two: Partners

Part Three: Allies
Part Four: Comrades
Total approx 63,000 words
Read more at https://www.simone-leigh.com/.

Also by Simone Leigh

Bought by the Billionaire
The Master's Maid
The Master's Contract
The Master's Courtesan
The Master's Desires
The Master's Fantasies
The Master's Obsession
The Master's Sin
The Master's Heart
The Master's Rage
The Master's Wife
The Master's Wife's Birthday

Bought by the Billionaire Box Set
Bought by the Billionaire. Box Set One. Books 1-6
The Master Series. Box Set 2. Books 7-10

Buying the Virgin
The Virgin Auctioned
The Virgin - Sold

The Virgin No More
The Virgin Unleashed
The Virgin Fulfilled
The Virgin's Holiday
The Virgin's Christmas
The Virgin's Valentines
The Virgin's Master
The Virgin's Lover
The Virgin's Fantasies
The Virgin's Choices
The Virgin's Summer - Part One
The Virgin's Summer - Part Two
The Virgin's Summer - Part Three
The Virgin and the Masters - Part One
The Virgin and the Masters, Part Two
The Virgin and the Masters - Part Three
The Virgin and the Masters - Part Four
The Virgin and the Masters - Part Five
The Virgin and the Masters - Part Six
The Virgin's Wedding
The Virgin's Real Christmas
The Virgin's Summer - Part Four

Buying the Virgin Box Set
Buying the Virgin - Box Set One
Buying the Virgin - Box Set Two
Buying the Virgin - Box Set Three - The Virgin's Summer
Buying the Virgin - Box Set Four - The Virgin and the Masters

Call of the Wild

Freedom
Thralldom
Retribution
Revelation
Redemption
Call of the Wild - Box Set

Charlotte's Search
Her Master's Wedding
Her Lovers' Touch
The Sin of the Parent
The Daughter's Manumission
The Father's Betrayal
The Shadow of Obsession
The Loss of Innocence
Her Mother's Love
Her Enemy's Promise

Charlotte's Search - Box Set
Charlotte's Search - Box Set One
Charlotte's Search Box Set Two
'Charlotte's Search' Box Set Three

Kirstie's Tale
A Dream of White Horses
An Illusion of Happiness
The Gathering of Storm Clouds
A Conspiracy of Ravens

Mastering the Virgin
Friends
Partners
Allies
Comrades
Rivals
Lovers
Masters
Dominants
Suitors
Penitents
Confidants
Champions
Triad
Alphas
Guardians
Hunters
Saviours
Family

Mastering the Virgin Box Set
Mastering the Virgin - Box Set One
Mastering the Virgin Box Set Two
Mastering the Virgin - Box Set Three
Mastering the Virgin Box Set Four: A BDSM Ménage Erotic Thriller
Mastering the Virgin - Box Set Five

Submissive to Her Master

Enslaved
Enthralled
Entranced
Enticed
Submissive to Her Master - The Box Set

Tales of Blood and Darkness
White as Bone

The Master's Child
Target

Standalone
Hearts of Fire. Poems of Love, Romance and Erotica
Kirstie's Tale - The Box Set
Trio - Three Short Stories
Mastering Charlotte
Buying Charlotte - The Complete 'Buying the Virgin'

Watch for more at https://www.simone-leigh.com/.